# Lazarillo de Tormes

## Anonymous

## A Dual-Language Book

Edited and Translated by
STANLEY APPELBAUM

DOVER PUBLICATIONS, INC.
Mineola, New York

*Bibliographical Note*

This Dover edition, first published in 2001, contains the complete Spanish text of the work as originally published by Juan de Junta, Burgos, in 1554 (with modernized punctuation and certain other modifications; see the section "The Nature of This Edition" in the Introduction), together with the interpolations included in the edition printed by Salcedo, Alcalá de Henares, 1554; the Dover edition also contains a new English translation by Stanley Appelbaum, who provided the Introduction and the footnotes in English.

*Library of Congress Cataloging-in-Publication Data*

Lazarillo de Tormes. English & Spanish.
   Lazarillo de Tormes / anonymous = anónimo ; edited and translated by Stanley Appelbaum.
      p. cm. — (A dual-language book)
   ISBN 0-486-41431-0 (pbk.)
      1. Appelbaum, Stanley. II. Title. III. Series.

PQ6408 .E5 2001
863'.3—dc21

00-064342

Manufactured in the United States of America
Dover Publications, Inc., 31 East 2nd Street, Mineola, N.Y. 11501

# Contents

# INTRODUCTION

**Early Publication History; the Text.** Midway in the 16th century, that glorious era of Spanish prose—after the "escapist" novels of chivalry and romantic love, the reports of the first conquistadors, and the Erasmian works of morality and politics, but before the great pastoral novels and the writings of the mystics—there appeared a brief, simple work that was to remain a treasured gem of the national literature: *La vida de Lazarillo de Tormes: y de sus fortunas y adversidades* (The Life of Lazarillo de Tormes, and Concerning His Fortunes and Adversities).

Three different editions all appeared in 1554: one published by Juan de Junta in Burgos, one printed by Salcedo in Alcalá de Henares, and one published by Martín Nucio in Antwerp. (Well before the definitive Spanish conquest of Antwerp in 1585, it had been under Spanish regency, and it was an international publishing center with strong commercial ties to Spain.) Experts in the affiliations of variant texts of literary works have established that the Burgos edition is not more than one step removed from the putative very-first edition, whereas the Alcalá and Antwerp editions, resembling each other more closely than either of them resembles the Burgos, are a minimum of two steps removed from that very-first.

The Alcalá edition differs from the others in another, important way. Calling itself an expanded second printing, it contains several passages, ranging in length from a few words to a few pages, that are clearly willful interpolations into the text. These interpolations, composed in a somewhat different style, sometimes interrupt the main text in a jarring way, sometimes contradict it (in Chapter Five, Lázaro states unequivocally that he is going to narrate only one of his experiences with the indulgence seller, but the long Alcalá interpolation adds two more), and sometimes spell out implications of the main text in a more prolix and obvious way.

Most modern Spanish editions have chosen to follow the Burgos text more or less closely, as being the most reliable one, but they usually include the Alcalá interpolations in one form or another. This Dover edition follows Burgos extremely closely, and includes the interpolations (within square brackets, and signaled by footnotes) for the sake of completeness. (More details will be given below in the section "The Nature of This Edition.")

**Book Title and Chapter Headings.** At least one modern Spanish literary historian believes firmly that the book title, as well as the chapter divisions and headings, that appear in the 1554 editions are not original with the author of the novel. With regard to the title: the syntax is very awkward, and the hero is called Lazarillo only once in the text itself (the blind man calls him that when he is quite young); everywhere else (and when he is speaking of himself) he is called Lázaro. With regard to the chapter titles: not only do they unnecessarily divide a single epistle (the whole book) into sections of peculiarly varying lengths, but they are sometimes (especially in the last chapter, but also to an extent in the first) woefully inadequate as summaries of the contents. Other critics, however, defend the 1554 editions.

**Authorship.** Because no author's name appeared, and the style of the book was so outwardly simple, many early readers must have taken the work for what it purported to be: a letter written by Lázaro himself to a benevolent gentleman. But more careful readers concluded that the book was too subtle, well-constructed, and learned to be written by a town crier and assistant hangman, and as early as 1605 an unending series of attributions began. The very first, to a friar named Juan de Ortega, still has much to commend it, because of the author's obvious acquaintance with ecclesiastical matters: not only are most of Lázaro's masters and patrons churchmen, but the text is also liberally interlarded with references to the New Testament and to Church ritual. In 1607 the work was attributed to the eminent diplomat, historian, and poet Diego Hurtado de Mendoza (1503–1571), who was only the first of numerous major writers of the first half of the 16th century to be so honored. Many of the others were authors of treatises and tracts influenced by the great reformer of Church and state Desiderius Erasmus; the frequent criticisms of the clergy in the novel lent support to these ascriptions. In the 20th century a strong case, closely based on verbal parallels, was made for the satirist

Sebastián de Horozco (dates uncertain). But none of these arguments has ever convinced a majority of experts, and every edition still bears the notice "anonymous."[1]

**Dating.** Although the author may have set his story in a past distant by several decades, arguments about the dating of the novel often tie the date of composition rather closely to the date of the action. Two historical events mentioned in the book are matters of dispute: the raid on Los Gelves, in which Lázaro's mother says her husband perished, and the Emperor's parliament in Toledo, referred to at the very end of the book. Since there were raids on Los Gelves in 1510 and in 1525, and parliaments in Toledo in 1520 and 1538, there is still plenty of room for argument. Proponents of a date for *Lazarillo* substantially earlier than its 1554 editions point out that the 1510 raid on Los Gelves is much more likely to be meant, because it was long remembered as a national disaster; their opponents claim that Lázaro's mother was probably lying, anyway, in an attempt to shed glory on her husband's futile life and death. The supporters of an earlier 16th-century date also interpret a casual reference to the king of France as meaning the captivity of François I after the battle of Pavia; but their strongest suit is the anticlerical bias of the story, which they claim links it to the above-mentioned Spanish Erasmians.

A very carefully reasoned recent view, based on a variety of historical data, places both the date of composition and the date of the action very close to 1554. To mention only two of the many convincing arguments: a law was passed in Toledo outlawing beggars from outside the city in 1546, and Valladolid was enjoying a real-estate boom in the 1540s and 1550s, thanks to the presence of the royal court there in those years; both these facts are faithfully reflected in the third chapter of the novel. According to this plausible theory, the date of the action is close to the date of composition; the book was written sometime between 1551 and 1553, and the lost ultra-first edition was published in 1553.

**The Continuations.** There are several indications that the unknown author intended the book to be completely self-standing and

---

1. The geography of the story affords no cogent clue, either. Extremely little is said about Salamanca and the towns between it and Toledo (although every detail that *is* given is verifiable). The author seems fairly well acquainted with Toledo, even noting the steepness of its streets (everyone walks "up" or "down"), but this doesn't furnish sufficient evidence.

end-stopped. Among these is the way in which the final chapter, in which the hero is settled for life, picks up verbal strands (almost leit-motifs) from the opening chapter: like his mother, Lázaro now wants to "throw in his lot with good people," and his position as assistant hangman is linked to his father's punishment for stealing grain by the same humorous reference to the Sermon on the Mount, about suffering persecution for the sake of righteousness. Nevertheless, continuations seem to have proved irresistible, perhaps because the very last interpolation in the 1554 Alcalá edition (the closing words of the story) had opened the door wide to them.

A 1555 edition included a second part that was certainly not by the original author. In the course of this fantasy, Lázaro joins German soldiers at the Emperor's court on an expedition against Algiers. When they are shipwrecked, he is transformed into a tuna and has many undersea adventures with the King of the Fish. Caught in a net, he regains his human form and returns to Salamanca.

Much more highly regarded literarily is the continuation by Juan de Luna published in 1620. Again, Lázaro is headed for Algiers, but on the way he meets his former noble master again at Cartagena. After they are shipwrecked together, Lázaro is caught by fishermen, who exhibit him all over Spain as a freak. Escaping, he returns to Toledo, where he finds that the rumors about his wife and the archpriest were all too true. He works as a porter in Madrid and has many other strange adventures. The book, safely published in Paris, is extremely anticlerical and anti-Inquisition. Other close imitations of *Lazarillo de Tormes* continued to appear well into the 17th century.

The original *Lazarillo* itself was banned by the Inquisition in 1559, but its popularity was so great that an edition lacking many of the negative references to the clergy and highest nobility was permitted to appear in 1573 under the title *Lazarillo castigado*.

**Views of the Novel's Meaning and Significance.** Both in its contents and its fortunes, *Lazarillo* was a sort of hinge between the reign of Charles I (Holy Roman Emperor Charles V), in which it was still possible to state some liberal opinions and to criticize authorities, and the fanatically repressive reign of his son Philip II, which began in 1556. The book is written in the form of a single epistle addressed to an unnamed gentleman, a well-wisher of Lázaro's who has asked him to elaborate on a specific matter (*caso*), no doubt the rumored infidelity of Lázaro's wife, which is also called a *caso* in the last chapter. Lázaro chooses to delve far back into his childhood to clarify and

amplify the matter. Thus, in a way that was novel for the time, the pro-
logue is not merely a preamble, but is tied directly in with the principal story line.

To this day, there are optimistic and pessimistic views of the novel's
meaning. The writer of the article about the book in a recent and
readily accessible English-language reference work still believes
Lázaro's own words implicitly, blithely overlooking the unknown author's deep, pervasive irony: this article writer believes that the blind
man was a benevolent educator of the boy *in loco parentis,* and that at
the end Lázaro is truly blissfully happy in his work and home life. The
pessimists, who have much more in their favor, see the book as the
story of a botched life: Lázaro leaves his broken home only to be ed-
ucated in the ways of deception and roguery, and to end up as a despised member of society and a complacent cuckold. Other pessimists
see the book, persuasively, as an indictment of the state of Spain at the
time, with its gross inequalities in the distribution of wealth, its all-
but-bankrupt economy, its swarms of beggars, the foolish pride of its
nobles, and the degradation of its clergy.[2]

Even though *Lazarillo* was influenced by earlier Spanish literature
(see the section "The Picaresque Genre," below), and though large
and small plot elements may derive from the ancient writers Lucian
and Apuleius (*The Golden Ass* may have provided the overall concept
of a suffering servant passing from one master to another), there is no
doubt of the fundamental originality of many features of our anonymous novel. If not the first realistic novel of everyday lower-class life,
it is surely one of the earliest examples, and its emphasis on the child-
that-makes-the-man is extremely impressive for its time. The clarity
and lack of rhetorical pomposity of its style (though the author rel-
ishes the kind of puns and word play that would later characterize
*Don Quixote* and many other Spanish classics) is also new and re-
freshing. The book has also long been famous in manuals of literature
as the first picaresque novel, the forefather of that genre so typical of
Spain (see the section "The Picaresque Genre," below).

**The Characters.** Lázaro (who is probably not a long-standing folk
figure, as has sometimes been claimed), as the omnipresent narrator,
is easily the most well-rounded character. Even though his childish
innocence is literally knocked out of him at a very early stage, he

---

2. Even the chaplain of Chapter Six, who may seem innocent, isn't really so, because it was improper for him to "moonlight" as a water-vending entrepreneur.

remains likable, his roguery being a means of survival. He is kind to his baby half-brother and feels compassion (a literary first?) for his impecunious noble master. He caps his career as an antihero by simply deserting his constabulary duties at a critical moment. Both parts of his name are meaningful: Lázaro refers to the perpetually hungry beggar in Luke 16, while "de Tormes" refers to his birth "in the river," which forecasts the mobility and impermanence of his existence.[3] Thanks to the novel, *lazarillo* has entered the Spanish language as the designation of a guide to the blind.

The crafty, malevolent blind man is a traditional figure in medieval and later European literature. One of his literary descendants evokes horror in Luis Buñuel's 1950 film *Los olvidados* ("The Forgotten Ones," a.k.a. "The Young and the Damned").

The nobleman of Chapter Three is the figure dearest to the heart of Spanish critics, who like that chapter best.[4] He is an *escudero,* originally a knight's assistant ("shield-bearer"), but at this period practically synonymous with *hidalgo,* the lowest level of nobility, beneath the knight (*caballero*) and the grandee (*grande*). By the time of the novel, the grandees and the highest prelates had cornered the nation's wealth (much of which was squandered on luxury imports and military adventures, so that even the gold shipments from the New World couldn't turn the tide), and the *hidalgos,* not permitted to labor even if their ancestral pride permitted it, were largely impoverished.

The Order of La Merced to which the friar of Chapter Four belongs was founded in the early 13th century with the primary purpose of arranging the ransom of Christians in Muslim captivity in North Africa. By the 16th century, however, the Mercedarians were a byword for corruption and loose living.

What Lázaro's fifth master, the indulgence seller (*buldero*), is actually selling is copies of Papal bulls (*bulas*) that grant the purchaser an indulgence, a reduction of the time that his soul must remain in Purgatory. The specific bulls referred to were due to a deal between Emperor Charles V and the Papacy. The ostensible purpose was to finance a crusade against the Ottoman Turks, who had been harrying southeastern Europe since their conquest of Constantinople in 1453. In reality, these bulls were tantamount to an additional tax on the

---

3. The editor of this edition has seen no discussion of this "birth in the river" anywhere in print.   4. That chapter certainly is related in loving detail, every incident being lingered over; but it is possible to prefer the youthful freshness of the first chapter, whereas, from the standpoint of unity and plotting, the second chapter, recounting Lázaro's single-minded war with the breadbox, wins hands down.

population: the collection of the proceeds was government-regulated, and was farmed out to private "commissioners" who paid a fixed fee and then raked in as much money as they could; parishioners were compelled by law to attend the promotional sermons delivered by the itinerant vendors of the bulls. The indulgence seller in the novel is apparently an even lower form of scoundrel, who is hawking absolute fakes and is utterly unscrupulous in his methods.

Lázaro's other masters are inconsequential, or exist only as one-dimensional types: the priest of Chapter Two, for instance, merely represents miserliness.

Aside from Lázaro himself, the only admirable characters are found among the lowliest of the lowly. The mutual devotion of the members of his mother's second family is touching, and it is the next-door neighbor women in Chapter Three who keep Lázaro alive, although they possess nothing and are "no better than they should be" (apparently they are at the sexual beck and call of the Mercedarian friar).

**The Picaresque Genre.** The word *pícaro* (no truly satisfactory etymology has ever been proposed) seems to have first appeared in writing in 1525, denoting a kitchen boy. By 1545 it had acquired its lasting meaning as someone of evil habits, a rogue or scoundrel. (The word appears nowhere in *Lazarillo de Tormes.*) From about 1600 on, stories of *pícaros* and *pícaras* became a more or less well-defined genre of Spanish fiction, not to say one of its most characteristic glories.

As the genre is usually defined, a rogue narrates in the first person a string of unsavory adventures among criminals as he wanders unstably from place to place. The earliest and best picaresque novels, it is said, still dwell on the antihero's psychology, while the later ones tend to become mere adventure novels, but of low life.

Is *Lazarillo de Tormes* a true picaresque novel, or merely the early inspiration for the genre? If it actually is one, is it the earliest? Opinions have differed widely. Incidents involving lower-class rogues, especially bawds and their hangers-on, are to be found here and there in medieval Spanish literature, and one of the greatest bawds in world literature is the title character in Fernando de Rojas's classic novel-in-dialogue *La Celestina*[5] (1499; expanded version, 1501).

---

5. Throughout this section, the customary short titles of novels are given for convenience. For instance, *La Celestina* is actually titled *Tragicomedia de Calisto y Melibea*, and *La Lozana andaluza* is actually titled *Retrato de la Lozana andaluza.*

A strong contender for the appellation "first picaresque novel" is Francisco Delicado's novel-in-dialogue *La Lozana andaluza* (Lozana of Andalusia; 1528), in which a willful girl from Córdoba becomes a leading courtesan and madam in Rome. This no-holds-barred novel also includes a male character named Rampín, Lozana's servant and lover, who shares a few characteristics with the later Lázaro.

When the great early picaresque novels that followed *Lazarillo* (as opposed to the flock of imitators and coattail-riders) are examined more carefully, they exhibit such strong individual features (sometimes negating the generic definition of this novelistic subclass) that it behooves the historian to adopt a more fluid and open-ended view of the genre.

After a 45-year hiatus following *Lazarillo* (explainable by the unfavorable circumstances of the repressive reign of Philip II) came the picaresque novel par excellence, the one that best fits the generic definition and that should possibly be regarded as the true founder, rather than precursor, of the genre: *Guzmán de Alfarache* (Part One, 1599; Part Two, 1605) by Mateo Alemán (1547–1614?). Guzmán is truly an antisocial crook who leaves his wretched home as a boy to become a gambler, thief, impostor, and con man. He ends up in the galleys after roaming widely through Spain and Italy. (As the genre progresses, *pícaros* cover more and more geographical territory, a far cry from the 100-odd miles that Lázaro walks between Salamanca and Toledo.)

In *La pícara Justina* (1605; by Francisco López de Úbeda?) the protagonist is a woman (as in the *Lozana* of 1528 and a number of later 17th-century novels).

In *Marcos de Obregón* (1618) by Vicente Espinel (1550–1624) the hero does rub elbows with the commonest folk, and isn't above practicing deceptions, but he is of better family and far less of a rogue. He studies at the university in Salamanca, and is imprisoned in Algiers; he doesn't come to a bad end.

By far the most distinguished known author of a picaresque novel is the great poet and prose writer Francisco de Quevedo y Villegas (1580–1645), one of the glories of Spain's Golden Age. In his *Buscón* (Swindler; 1626), the hero, Don Pablos, attends the university in Alcalá, but is put upon by rich students (his own family is quite déclassé: his father is hanged, and his uncle is an executioner). He learns to steal and play wild pranks. After numerous scapegrace adventures in various Spanish cities, he leaves for the West Indies.

*El diablo cojuelo* (The Lame Devil; 1641) by Luis Vélez de Guevara

(1579–1644) is not narrated in the first person, and its hero is not a rogue, but a student who unknowingly frees a devil from his confinement in a flask. The devil shows him the secret goings-on at many locales in Spain. A satirical look at society, including the dealings of *pícaros*, is thus combined with fantasy not typical of the genre.

In the anonymous *Estebanillo González* (1646) the amoral hero encounters numerous adventures in Flanders, Germany, Poland, and Italy, as a servant of many masters, as a buffoon to grandees, and as a gambler.

The picaresque atmosphere of the late 16th and early 17th centuries affected other writers who didn't make the genre their sole or chief interest. Some of Cervantes's best *Novelas ejemplares* (Exemplary Stories; 1613) concern *pícaros*, and Part One of *Don Quixote* (1605) contains some notable rogues, especially the first innkeeper (Chapters II and III) and the galley convicts (Chapter XXII), one of whom even refers specifically to *Lazarillo de Tormes*.

The picaresque impulse had spent itself in Spain by 1700, but it was given new life elsewhere in the 18th century. The French writer Alain-René Lesage (1668–1747) adapted *El diablo cojuelo* as *Le diable boiteux* (1707) and created an exciting new *pícaro*, on Spanish models, in *Gil Blas de Santillane* (Part One, 1715; Part Two, 1735). In England, Tobias Smollett (1721–1771) carried on the tradition with such novels as *Roderick Random* (1748) and *Peregrine Pickle* (1751), as did Henry Fielding (1707–1754) with *Tom Jones* (1749). In the United States, Mark Twain's *Huckleberry Finn* (1884) has been called the nearest equivalent to *Lazarillo de Tormes*.

**The Nature of This Edition.** In common with most modern editions, the Spanish text in this volume is based on the 1554 Burgos edition, which it follows even more closely than many other editions do, adopting the Burgos readings even when they are more difficult or problematic and make the translation a little more awkward; only obvious typographical errors are altered. For the sake of completeness, the 1554 Alcalá interpolations are included (in square brackets and signaled by footnotes in English) in both the Spanish text and the translation. (Not every English translation has included them.)

In accordance with every Spanish edition known to us, the Burgos punctuation has been thoroughly modernized; this includes sentence breaks and paragraph breaks.

With regard to spelling, modern Spanish editions exhibit a range of choices that extends from a complete retention of the 1554 spelling to

the most thoroughgoing modernization of every form of every word. The most up-to-date editions adopt a mixed policy, modernizing certain elements but retaining others, sometimes with the clear purpose of preserving old word forms, at other times with obscurer motives that may involve the preservation of conjectural 16th-century pronunciations. This Dover edition, perhaps somewhat arbitrarily, preserves certain recognizable old forms (so as not to misrepresent the fact that we are dealing with a 450-year-old text) but modernizes words that seem merely to exhibit an older spelling based on etymology, and might needlessly confuse a nonspecialist reader, with little to be gained in return.

Thus, in common with the above-mentioned up-to-date Spanish editions, we retain forms like *ansí, agora, dende, fasta, planto, mirá,* and *castigaldo* (equivalent to modern *así, ahora, desde, hasta, llanto, mirad,* and *castigadlo*), but, unlike them, we replace forms like *acaesció, caxco, sancto, Sant,* and *dubda* by their modern forms *acaesció, casco, santo, San,* and *duda.*

There have been numerous English translations of the novel since as early as 1576, but the editor is unaware of prior dual-language editions. This new translation into modern American English strives to be as full and as accurate as possible. Five annotated Spanish editions and two earlier English translations have been consulted. The text is so idiomatic, and so many semantic changes have occurred since 1554, that it would be extremely foolhardy to promise total accuracy (occasional odd lapses even in otherwise first-rate earlier translations are a solemn warning), but the attempt has been consciously made. (Even Spanish literary historians disagree on the specific connotations of many a passage; some major instances are cited in footnotes.)

Another feature of the original text is its unflagging humor, frequently taking the form of puns and word plays. Wherever possible, the English translation offers an equivalent, but when this was altogether impossible, or the meaning would have had to be unduly strained, the word play is pointed out in a footnote.

In addition to the two uses just mentioned, the footnotes supply concise explanations of historical, geographical, and cultural references, and a miscellany of other information and commentary.

# Lazarillo de Tormes

# Prólogo

Yo por bien tengo que cosas tan señaladas y por ventura nunca oídas ni vistas vengan a noticia de muchos y no se entierren en la sepultura del olvido, pues podría ser que alguno que las lea halle algo que le agrade, y a los que no ahondaren tanto los deleite. Y a este propósito dice Plinio que no hay libro, por malo que sea, que no tenga alguna cosa buena. Mayormente que los gustos no son todos unos, mas lo que uno no come, otro se pierde por ello; y así vemos cosas tenidas en poco de algunos, que de otros no lo son. Y esto para que ninguna cosa se debría romper, ni echar a mal, si muy detestable no fuese, sino que a todos se comunicase, mayormente siendo sin perjuicio y pudiendo sacar della algún fruto; porque, si así no fuese, muy pocos escribirían para uno solo, pues no se hace sin trabajo, y quieren, ya que lo pasan, ser recompensados, no con dineros, mas con que vean y lean sus obras, y si hay de qué, se las alaben. Y a este propósito dice Tulio: "La honra cría las artes."

¿Quién piensa que el soldado que es primero del escala, tiene más aborrecido el vivir? No por cierto; mas el deseo de alabanza le hace ponerse al peligro. Y así en las artes y letras es lo mesmo. Predica muy bien el presentado, y es hombre que desea mucho el provecho de las ánimas; mas pregunten a su merced si le pesa cuando le dicen: "¡Oh qué maravillosamente lo ha hecho vuestra reverencia!" Justó muy ruinmente el señor don Fulano, y dio el sayete de armas al truhán porque le loaba de haber llevado muy buenas lanzas. ¿Qué hiciera si fuera verdad?

# Prologue

I find it only right that matters so exceptional,[1] and perhaps[2] never before heard or seen, should come to the attention of the public and not be buried in the grave of oblivion, because someone reading them might very well find something congenial in them, and some aspect of them might entertain those who don't delve so deeply. And, in connection with this, Pliny[3] says that there's no book, bad as it may be, which doesn't have some good quality. Especially because not all tastes are the same, but what one man won't eat, another man is wild for; and so we see things disparaged by some people that aren't by others. And therefore nothing should be torn up and thrown away, unless it's extremely objectionable, but everything should be made known to everyone, especially if it's harmless and some advantage can be derived from it. Because, if that weren't so, very few authors would write for an audience of one, since a book isn't written without toil, and, if they undergo this, they want to be rewarded, not with money, but by having their works seen and read, and praised if they deserve it. On this subject, Cicero says: "The quest for reputation creates the arts."[4]

Who imagines that the soldier who is first to scale a wall in a siege is the one who most hates life? Not at all: it's the yearning for praise that makes him expose himself to danger. And it's the same in the arts and letters. The divinity graduate seeking an appointment delivers a fine sermon, and he's a man who is very eager for the welfare of his listeners' souls; but let them ask the gentleman if it annoys him to have people say: "Oh, what a wonderful job your reverence did!" Sir What's-his-name performed terribly in a joust, but he made his buffoon a gift of the doublet he wore beneath his armor because the buffoon praised him for wielding his lances wonderfully. What would he have done if it were true?

---

1. Or: "so often criticized." 2. Or: "fortunately." 3. In one of his letters, the Roman author Pliny the Younger (*c.* A.D. 61–*c.* 112) attributes this remark to his uncle, the encyclopedist Pliny the Elder (A.D. 23–79). 4. The Roman statesman, orator, and philosopher (106–43 B.C.) makes this remark in his *Tusculan Disputations.*

Y todo va desta manera: que confesando yo no ser más santo que mis vecinos, desta nonada, que en este grosero estilo escribo, no me pesará que hayan parte y se huelguen con ello todos los que en ella algún gusto hallaren, y vean que vive un hombre con tantas fortunas, peligros y adversidades.

Suplico a Vuestra Merced reciba el pobre servicio de mano de quien lo hiciera más rico si su poder y deseo se conformaran. Y pues Vuestra Merced escribe se le escriba y relate el caso muy por extenso, parecióme no tomalle por el medio, sino del principio, porque se tenga entera noticia de mi persona, y también porque consideren los que heredaron nobles estados cuán poco se les debe, pues Fortuna fue con ellos parcial, y cuánto más hicieron los que, siéndoles contraria, con fuerza y maña remando salieron a buen puerto.

# TRATADO PRIMERO

## Cuenta Lázaro su vida
## y cúyo hijo fue

Pues sepa Vuestra Merced ante todas cosas que a mí llaman Lázaro de Tormes, hijo de Tomé Gonzales y de Antona Pérez, naturales de Tejares, aldea de Salamanca. Mi nacimiento fue dentro del río Tormes, por la cual causa tomé el sobrenombre, y fue desta manera: mi padre, que Dios perdone, tenía cargo de proveer una molienda de una aceña que está ribera de aquel río, en la cual fue molinero más de quince años; y estando mi madre una noche en la aceña, preñada de mí, tomóle el parto y parióme allí; de manera que con verdad me puedo decir nacido en el río.

Pues siendo yo niño de ocho años, achacaron a mi padre ciertas sangrías mal hechas en los costales de los que allí a moler venían, por lo cual fue preso, y confesó, y no negó, y padeció persecución por justicia. Espero en Dios que está en la Gloria, pues el Evangelio los llama bienaventurados. En este tiempo se hizo cierta armada contra moros, entre los cuales fue mi padre, que a la sazón estaba desterrado por el desastre ya dicho, con

And everything works the same way. Though I confess that I'm no holier than my neighbors, I won't be sorry if all those who might take some pleasure in this trifle, which I'm writing in this crude style, will come to know it and enjoy it, and if they see that a man can survive so many misfortunes, perils, and adversities.

I beseech Your Honor to accept this poor handiwork of one who would make you richer if his power were as great as his wishes. And since Your Honor has written me requesting me to write to you and narrate the matter in great detail, I felt that I shouldn't start in the middle, but begin at the beginning, so that you may become fully acquainted with me, and, in addition, so that those who have inherited noble rank may judge how little that is due to their own merits, since Fortune favored them, and how much more was accomplished by those who, finding Fortune hostile to them, reached a safe haven by rowing with strength and skill.

## CHAPTER ONE

## Lázaro Tells the Story of His Life and Whose Son He Was

Well, Your Honor should know first of all that I'm called Lázaro of Tormes, son of Tomé Gonzales and Antona Pérez, natives of Tejares, a village just outside Salamanca. My birth took place within the river Tormes, on account of which I adopted this surname, and it happened this way: My father, may God forgive him, was assigned to supervising the grinding of grain at a water mill located on the banks of that river; he was miller there for more than fifteen years. One night when my mother, pregnant with me, was in the mill, she was seized with her labor pains and gave birth to me there. And so I can truly say I was born in the river.

Well, when I was a boy of eight, my father was accused of some careless "blood-lettings" in the sacks of those who brought their grain to be ground there. On that account he was arrested, confessed and didn't deny it, and suffered punishment at the hands of justice. I hope to God that he's in glory, because the Gospel says that those who are persecuted for the sake of justice are blessed. At that time a certain naval expedition was mounted against the Moors,[5] and my father was

---

5. In 1494, the Pope, generously dividing up the world among the explorer nations, gave much of North Africa to the Spaniards, who needed only to conquer it! They made many raids in the course of the 16th century.

cargo de acemilero de un caballero que allá fue; y con su señor, como leal criado, feneció su vida.

Mi viuda madre, como sin marido y sin abrigo se viese, determinó arrimarse a los buenos por ser uno dellos, y vínose a vivir a la ciudad, y alquiló una casilla, y metióse a guisar de comer a ciertos estudiantes, y lavaba la ropa a ciertos mozos de caballos del Comendador de la Magdalena; de manera que fue frecuentando las caballerizas.

Ella y un hombre moreno, de aquellos que las bestias curaban, vinieron en conocimiento. Este algunas veces se venía a nuestra casa, y se iba a la mañana; otras veces de día llegaba a la puerta, en achaque de comprar huevos, y entrábase en casa. Yo, al principio de su entrada, pesábame con él y habíale miedo, viendo el color y mal gesto que tenía; mas de que vi que con su venida mejoraba el comer, fuile queriendo bien, porque siempre traía pan, pedazos de carne, y en el invierno leños, a que nos calentábamos.

De manera que, continuando la posada y conversación, mi madre vino a darme un negrito muy bonito, el cual yo brincaba y ayudaba a calentar. Y acuérdome que estando el negro de mi padrastro trebajando con el mozuelo, como el niño vía a mi madre y a mí blancos, y a él no, huía dél con miedo para mi madre, y señalando con el dedo decía: "¡Madre, coco!" Respondió él riendo: "¡Hideputa!" Yo, aunque bien mochacho, noté aquella palabra de mi hermanico, y dije entre mí: "¡Cuántos debe de haber en el mundo que huyen de otros porque no se veen a sí mesmos!"

Quiso nuestra fortuna que la conversación del Zaide, que así se llamaba, llegó a oídos del mayordomo, y hecha pesquisa, hallóse que la mitad por medio de la cebada que para las bestias le daban hurtaba; y salvados, leña, almohazas, mandiles, y las mantas y sábanas de los caballos hacía perdidas; y cuando otra cosa no tenía, las bestias desherraba, y con todo esto acudía a mi madre para criar a mi hermanico. No nos maravillemos de un clérigo ni fraile porque el uno hurta

among them,[6] being in exile at the time because of the above-mentioned misfortune. He was serving as a mule driver for a knight who was there; like a loyal servant, he died along with his master.

My widowed mother, finding herself without a husband or a roof over her head, decided to "throw in her lot with the good people, and so join their number." She moved into town, rented a little house, and began to cook meals for some of the university students; she also did laundry for some stable hands in the employ of the Knight Commander of the Church of the Magdalen,[7] so that she frequented the stables.[8] She and a black man, one of those who took care of the horses, got to know each other very well. Sometimes[9] he would come to our house and leave in the morning; other times he would come to our door in the daytime with the pretext of buying eggs, and would then come inside. When he first started visiting us, I disliked him and was afraid of him because of his color and his ugly face; but as soon as I realized that his visits meant better food for us, I grew to like him, because he always brought along bread, pieces of meat, and, in the wintertime, firewood for keeping us warm.

And so, as his stay with us and his intimacy with my mother continued, she finally presented me with a very cute little black brother, whom I used to dandle and help tuck in. And I remember that, once, when my unhappy[10] stepfather was playing with the little boy, the child, seeing that my mother and I were white but his father wasn't, was frightened by him, took refuge with my mother, and pointed at him, saying: "Mommy, the bogeyman!" Laughing, he replied: "You rascal!" Though I was still a boy, I took notice of what my little brother said, and I thought to myself: "How many people there must be in the world who shun others because they can't see themselves!"

As our bad luck would have it, my mother's intimacy with Zaid, for that was his name, came to the attention of the Knight Commander's steward. When he investigated, it was discovered that my stepfather was stealing half of the barley he was given for the horses; he was pretending that bran, wood, currycombs, rubdown towels, and horse blankets and cloths were being lost. When he found nothing else to take, he used to unshoe the horses. He used all this to help my mother raise my little brother. Let's not be surprised when a priest steals from

---

6. At least one commentator, perhaps over-subtly, believes that the ambiguous Spanish wording implies a joke on the author's part that Lázaro's father was himself a Moor (a *morisco*, or convert).   7. This church in Salamanca was the property of the knightly order of Alcántara.   8. This may imply that she was a cheap prostitute.   9. Or "some nights," if, as some editors believe, the Spanish *algunas veces* is an error for *algunas noches.*   10. With a pun on "black."

de los pobres, y el otro de casa para sus devotas y para ayuda de otro tanto, cuando a un pobre esclavo el amor le animaba a esto.

Y probósele cuanto digo y aun más, porque a mí, con amenazas, me preguntaban, y como niño respondía y descubría cuanto sabía con miedo, hasta ciertas herraduras que por mandado de mi madre a un herrero vendí. Al triste de mi padrastro azotaron y pringaron, y a mi madre pusieron pena por justicia, sobre el acostumbrado centenario, que en casa del sobredicho Comendador no entrase ni al lastimado Zaide en la suya acogiese.

Por no echar la soga tras el caldero, la triste se esforzó y cumplió la sentencia; y por evitar peligro y quitarse de malas lenguas, se fue a servir a los que al presente vivían en el mesón de la Solana; y allí, padeciendo mil importunidades, se acabó de criar mi hermanico hasta que supo andar, y a mí hasta ser buen mozuelo, que iba a los huéspedes por vino y candelas y por lo demás que me mandaban.

En este tiempo vino a posar al mesón un ciego, el cual, pareciéndole que yo sería para adestralle, me pidió a mi madre, y ella me encomendó a él diciéndole cómo era hijo de un buen hombre, el cual, por ensalzar la fe, había muerto en la de los Gelves, y que ella confiaba en Dios no saldría peor hombre que mi padre, y que le rogaba me tratase bien y mirase por mí, pues era huérfano. Él respondió que así lo haría y que me recibía no por mozo, sino por hijo. Y así le comencé a servir y adestrar a mi nuevo y viejo amo.

Como estuvimos en Salamanca algunos días, pareciéndole a mi amo que no era la ganancia a su contento, determinó irse de allí, y cuando nos hubimos de partir yo fui a ver a mi madre, y ambos llorando, me dio su bendición y dijo: —Hijo, ya sé que no te veré más; procura de ser bueno, y Dios te guíe; criado te he y con buen amo te he puesto, válete por ti.

Y así, me fui para mi amo, que esperándome estaba. Salimos de Salamanca, y llegando a la puente, está a la entrada

the poorbox to support his sweethearts, or when a friar plunders his monastery to help out his own "lady devotees,"[11] if a poor slave was emboldened to do this out of love.

All the charges against him that I've mentioned, and more, were proved, because they interrogated me with threats and, child that I was, my fear led me to answer and reveal all I knew, even confessing that, at my mother's request, I had sold some horseshoes to a blacksmith. My unfortunate stepfather was flogged and had hot fat dripped onto his wounds. My mother's sentence, over and above the usual hundred lashes,[12] was never again to enter the house of the above-mentioned Knight Commander nor to receive the wounded Zaid in her own house.

So as not to make a bad matter worse,[13] the unhappy woman took heart and complied with the sentence. In order to avoid danger and free herself from slander, she became a servant of the people who were then running the Solana tavern.[14] There, suffering a thousand annoyances, she managed to raise my little brother until he could walk, and me until I was quite a big boy. I used to fetch wine and candles for the customers, and whatever else they sent me for.

At that time a blind man came to stay at the inn. Thinking I would make a suitable guide for him, he asked my mother for me. She entrusted me to him, telling him that I was the son of a good man who, in an effort to exalt our religion, had died on the expedition to Los Gelves;[15] she trusted in God that I wouldn't turn out to be a worse man than my father, and she asked him to treat me well and look after me, because I was an orphan. He answered that he would, and that he was taking me on not as a servant but as a son. And so I began to serve and guide my master, who was both new and old.

After we had been in Salamanca several days, my master felt that he wasn't earning as much as he would like, and he decided to leave. When we were to set out, I went to see my mother. We both wept, and she gave me her blessing, saying: "Son, I know now that I'll never see you again. Try to be a good boy, and may God direct your ways. I've brought you up and I've placed you with a good master. Take care of yourself."

And so I went to meet my master, who was waiting for me. We left Salamanca and came to the bridge. At the city end of it, there's a stone

---

11. This sentence, very ambiguous in the original, has been interpreted in a surprisingly large number of ways.    12. As a "heretic" cohabiting with a non-Christian. At least two Spanish editors have thought that Zaid was hanged; neither one was worried about the prohibition to receive him!    13. Literally: "to throw away the rope after losing the cauldron."    14. Located in the Salamanca city hall.    15. An island near Tunis, site of a raid, disastrous to the Spanish, in 1510.

della un animal de piedra, que casi tiene forma de toro, y el ciego mandóme que llegase cerca del animal, y allí puesto, me dijo: —Lázaro, llega el oído a este toro y oirás gran ruido dentro dél.

Yo simplemente llegué, creyendo ser ansí; y como sintió que tenía la cabeza par de la piedra, afirmó recio la mano y diome una gran calabazada en el diablo del toro, que más de tres días me duró el dolor de la cornada, y díjome: —Necio, aprende, que el mozo del ciego un punto ha de saber más que el diablo.

Y rió mucho la burla. Parecióme que en aquel instante desperté de la simpleza en que, como niño, dormido estaba. Dije entre mí: "Verdad dice éste, que me cumple avivar el ojo y avisar, pues solo soy, y pensar cómo me sepa valer."

Comenzamos nuestro camino, y en muy pocos días me mostró jerigonza; y como me viese de buen ingenio, holgábase mucho y decía: "Yo oro ni plata no te lo puedo dar; mas avisos para vivir muchos te mostraré." Y fue ansí, que, después de Dios, éste me dio la vida, y siendo ciego me alumbró y adestró en la carrera de vivir. Huelgo de contar a Vuestra Merced estas niñerías para mostrar cuánta virtud sea saber los hombres subir siendo bajos, y dejarse bajar siendo altos cuánto vicio.

Pues tornando al bueno de mi ciego y contando sus cosas, Vuestra Merced sepa que desde que Dios crió el mundo, ninguno formó más astuto ni sagaz. En su oficio era un águila: ciento y tantas oraciones sabía de coro; un tono bajo, reposado y muy sonable, que hacía resonar la iglesia donde rezaba; un rostro humilde y devoto, que con muy buen continente ponía cuando rezaba, sin hacer gestos ni visajes con boca ni ojos como otros suelen hacer. Allende desto, tenía otras mil formas y maneras para sacar el dinero. Decía saber oraciones para muchos y diversos efectos: para mujeres que no parían, para las que estaban de parto, para las que eran malcasadas, que sus maridos las quisiesen bien. Echaba pronósticos a las preñadas si traía hijo o hija. Pues en caso de medicina, decía que Galeno no supo la mitad que él para muela, desmayos, males de madre. Finalmente, nadie le decía padecer alguna pasión, que luego no le

figure of an animal, that looks something like a bull.[16] The blind man ordered me to go up to the animal. When I was standing there, he said: "Lázaro, put your ear next to this bull, and you'll hear a big noise inside it."

In my naïveté, I did so, believing what he said. When he sensed that my head was alongside the stone, he stiffened his hand and knocked my head hard against that damned bull, so that the pain of the "goring" lasted more than three days, and he said: "Dumbbell, learn that a blind man's boy needs to know a little more than the Devil does."

And he had a good laugh over his trick. I felt that at that very moment I awoke from the naïveté in which I had been childishly sleeping. I said to myself: "He's speaking the truth: it's up to me to keep my eyes peeled and to stay alert, because I'm alone in the world, and to plan how to look after myself."

We began our journey, and in a very few days he taught me his professional jargon; finding that I was a bright boy, he was very pleased, and he'd say: "I can't give you gold or silver, but I can give you plenty of advice on how to live." And so, after God, this man gave me life again and, though blind, he illumined and guided me on my path through existence. I take the time to recount these childish matters to Your Honor to show you what a great virtue it is when men of low condition are able to rise in life, and what a great vice it is when people high up let themselves slip down.

Well, to get back to my good blind man and to tell you about him, Your Honor should know that ever since God created the world, He never fashioned a shrewder or wiser man. He was an ace at his calling: he knew over a hundred prayers by heart; his voice was deep, calm, and very resonant, so that it rang through any church where he was praying; his face was humble and pious, and he controlled it carefully when he prayed, and didn't make grimaces and "faces" with his mouth or eyes as others generally do. In addition, he had a thousand other ways and means to get people's money. He told them that he knew prayers for many different purposes: for women who had no children, for those in childbirth, for those unhappily married, to make their husbands love them. He predicted to pregnant women whether they would have a boy or a girl. Then, when it came to curing, he said that Galen[17] didn't know half of what he did about toothache, fainting spells, and inflammations of the womb. Lastly, no one reported any

---

16. This Celtiberian bull or boar was put back on the Roman bridge in 1974 after a long absence.   17. Famous Greek physician of the second century A.D.

decía: "Haced esto, haréis estotro, coged tal yerba, tomad tal raíz." Con esto andábase todo el mundo tras él, especialmente mujeres, que cuanto les decía, creían. Déstas sacaba él grandes provechos con las artes que digo, y ganaba más en un mes que cien ciegos en un año.

Mas también quiero que sepa Vuestra Merced que con todo lo que adquiría y tenía, jamás tan avariento ni mezquino hombre no vi, tanto que me mataba a mí de hambre, y así no me demediaba de lo necesario. Digo verdad: si con mi sotileza y buenas mañas no me supiera remediar, muchas veces me finara de hambre; mas con todo su saber y aviso le contaminaba de tal suerte, que siempre, o las más veces, me cabía lo más y mejor. Para esto le hacía burlas endiabladas, de los cuales contaré algunas, aunque no todas a mi salvo.

Él traía el pan y todas las otras cosas en un fardel de lienzo que por la boca se cerraba con una argolla de hierro y su candado y su llave, y al meter de todas las cosas y sacallas, era con tan gran vigilancia y tanto por contadero, que no bastara hombre en todo el mundo hacerle menos una migaja. Mas yo tomaba aquella laceria que él me daba, la cual en menos de dos bocados era despachada. Después que cerraba el candado y se descuidaba, pensando que yo estaba entendiendo en otras cosas, por un poco de costura, que muchas veces del un lado del fardel descosía y tornaba a coser sangraba el avariento fardel, sacando no por tasa pan, mas buenos pedazos, torreznos y longaniza. Y ansí, buscaba conveniente tiempo para rehacer, no la chaza, sino la endiablada falta que el mal ciego me faltaba.

Todo lo que podía sisar y hurtar traía en medias blancas; y cuando le mandaban rezar y le daban blancas, como él carecía de vista, no había el que se la daba amagado con ella, cuando yo la tenía lanzada en la boca y la media aparejada, que por presto que él echaba la mano, ya iba de mi cambio aniquilada en la mitad del justo precio. Quejábaseme el mal ciego, porque al tiento luego conocía y sentía que no era blanca entera, y decía:

—¿Qué diablo es esto, que después que comigo estás no me

ailment to him without his replying at once: "Do this, do that, take[18] this herb, use this root." And so everyone trailed at his heels, especially the women, who believed everything he told them. He used to make great profit from them with the ruses I've mentioned, and he'd earn more in a month than a hundred other blind men did in a year.

But I also want Your Honor to know that, despite all that he made and owned, I never saw a greedier or stingier man, so much so that he used to kill me with hunger, and I never got even half of what I needed. I'm telling the truth: if I hadn't been able to help myself out with my cleverness and shrewd schemes, I would have perished of hunger many a time; but, despite all his knowledge and alertness, I fought back with so many ruses that I wound up with the most and the best always, or most of the time. In order to do this, I played mischievous tricks on him, some of which I'll tell you, though I didn't always get off scot-free.

He used to carry our bread and the rest of our supplies in a burlap sack, the opening of which was closed with an iron ring and which he kept under lock and key. When he put things in it or took them out, he was so vigilant and so meticulous that no one in the whole world could make him lose a crumb. And I used to take that miserable pittance he gave me, which was finished in less than two bites. After he fastened the lock and relaxed his guard, thinking that I was occupied with other things, I used to "bleed" that miserly sack through a small seam on one side of it that I would unsew and sew up again, taking not just a rationed portion of bread, but big pieces, as well as fried bacon and sausage. And so I'd wait for a suitable time—not to play the game again,[19] but to make up for that damned shortage which that mean blind man was causing me.

All that I could pilfer and steal I converted into half-*blanca* coins;[20] and when he was asked to pray and the people gave him *blanca* coins, since he couldn't see, the moment the donor handed one to me, I put it in my mouth[21] and had a half-*blanca* handy; so that, no matter how quickly he reached for it, it was already reduced to half its value at my rate of exchange. The nasty blind man used to complain to me, because he immediately knew and felt by touch that it wasn't a full *blanca*, and he'd say:

"What the devil is this? Ever since you've been with me, they give

---

18. All three 1554 editions have *cosed*, which must be interpreted as either *coged* or *coced* ("boil").   19. The Spanish sentence has several untranslatable puns, including terminology from the game of pelota.   20. The *blanca* was a very small denomination; two of them made one *maravedí*.   21. During the act of kissing it in gratitude.

dan sino medias blancas, y de antes una blanca y un maravedí hartas veces me pagaban? ¡En ti debe estar esta desdicha!

También él abreviaba el rezar y la mitad de la oración no acababa, porque me tenía mandado que, en yéndose el que la mandaba rezar, le tirase por cabo del capuz. Yo así lo hacía. Luego él tornaba a dar voces, diciendo: "¿Mandan rezar tal y tal oración?", como suelen decir.

Usaba poner cabe sí un jarrillo de vino cuando comíamos, y yo, muy de presto, le asía y daba un par de besos callados y tornábale a su lugar. Mas turóme poco, que en los tragos conocía la falta, y por reservar su vino a salvo, nunca después desamparaba el jarro, antes lo tenía por el asa asido. Mas no había piedra imán que así trajese a sí como yo con una paja larga de centeno, que para aquel menester tenía hecha, la cual metiéndola en la boca del jarro, chupando el vino lo dejaba a buenas noches. Mas como fuese el traidor tan astuto, pienso que me sintió, y dende en adelante mudó propósito, y asentaba su jarro entre las piernas, y atapábale con la mano, y ansí bebía seguro.

Yo, como estaba hecho al vino, moría por él; y viendo que aquel remedio de la paja no me aprovechaba ni valía, acordé en el suelo del jarro hacerle una fuentecilla y agujero sotil, y delicadamente con una muy delgada tortilla de cera taparlo, y al tiempo de comer, fingiendo haber frío, entrábame entre las piernas del triste ciego a calentarme en la pobrecilla lumbre que teníamos, y al calor della luego derretida la cera (por ser muy poca), comenzaba la fuentecilla a destilarme en la boca, la cual yo de tal manera ponía, que maldita la gota se perdía. Cuando el pobreto iba a beber, no hallaba nada. Espantábase, maldecíase, daba al diablo el jarro y el vino, no sabiendo qué podía ser.

—No diréis, tío, que os lo bebo yo —decía—, pues no le quitáis de la mano.

Tantas vueltas y tientos dio al jarro, que halló la fuente, y cayó en la burla; mas así lo disimuló como si no lo hubiera sentido. Y luego otro día, teniendo yo rezumando mi jarro como solía, no pensando el daño que me estaba aparejado ni que el mal ciego me sentía, sentéme como solía. Estando recibiendo aquellos dulces tragos, mi cara puesta hacia el cielo, un poco cerrados los

me only half-*blancas,* while previously they gave me a *blanca,* and many times a *maravedí.* This bad luck must be your fault!"

But he, too, used to shorten his prayers, stopping halfway, because he had ordered me to tug at the end of his cloak when the customer started to leave. And I did. Immediately the blind man would start calling out again: "Would you like me to recite such-and-such a prayer?", as their patter goes.

He used to place a little jug of wine at his side when we ate, and I very quickly grabbed it, gave it a couple of quiet "kisses," and put it back where it had been. But it didn't take him long to discover what was missing when he himself drank from it, and, to keep his wine safe, he never again let go of the jug, but held onto it by the handle. But no magnet ever attracted metal as strongly as I attracted that wine through a long rye straw I prepared for that purpose; putting it in the mouth of the jug and sucking out the wine, I left him in the dark with my trick.[22] But that villain was so clever that I think he heard me and, from that time on, he changed his plans, placing the jug between his legs, covering it with one hand, and thus drinking without worries.

Since I had grown used to the wine, I was dying for it; and, seeing that that recourse to the straw was of no use or help to me, it occurred to me to make a little "fountain," a small hole, in the bottom of the jug and to cover it delicately with a very thin layer of wax; at mealtime I would pretend to feel cold and would snuggle between the miserable blind man's legs to warm myself by the wretched little fire we had; as soon as its heat had melted the wax (which there wasn't much of), the little fountain began to trickle into my mouth, which I held in such a way that not a single drop was wasted. When the poor man went to drink, he would find nothing. He used to get frightened, curse himself, and commend the jug and the wine to the Devil, not knowing what could be wrong.

"'Uncle,' you can't say I'm drinking it on you," I would say, "because you don't take your hand off it."

He turned the jug around and felt it so often that he found the hole and realized he had been tricked. But he kept quiet about it just as if he hadn't become aware of it. On the very next day, while I was sucking at the jar in my regular way, unaware of the harm being prepared for me, not knowing that the nasty blind man heard me, I sat down in the usual manner. While I was taking those sweet gulps, with my face

---

22. A 14th-century Italian manuscript (illuminated in England?) depicts just such a scene, and contains other illustrations of a blind man and his young guide, perhaps based on popular plays of the time.

ojos por mejor gustar el sabroso licor, sintió el desesperado ciego que agora tenía tiempo de tomar de mí venganza, y con toda su fuerza, alzando con dos manos aquel dulce y amargo jarro, le dejó caer sobre mi boca, ayudándose, como digo, con todo su poder, de manera que el pobre Lázaro, que de nada desto se guardaba, antes, como otras veces, estaba descuidado y gozoso, verdaderamente me pareció que el cielo, con todo lo que en él hay, me había caído encima.

Fue tal el golpecillo, que me desatinó y sacó de sentido, y el jarrazo tan grande, que los pedazos dél se me metieron por la cara, rompiéndomela por muchas partes, y me quebró los dientes, sin los cuales hasta hoy día me quedé. Desde aquella hora quise mal al mal ciego; y aunque me quería y regalaba y me curaba, bien vi que se había holgado del cruel castigo. Lavóme con vino las roturas que con los pedazos del jarro me había hecho, y sonriéndose decía:

—¿Qué te parece, Lázaro? Lo que te enfermó te sana y da salud. —Y otros donaires, que a mi gusto no lo eran.

Ya que estuve medio bueno de mi negra trepa y cardenales, considerando que a pocos golpes tales el cruel ciego ahorraría de mí, quise yo ahorrar dél; mas no lo hice tan presto por hacello más a mi salvo y provecho. Y aunque yo quisiera asentar mi corazón y perdonalle el jarrazo, no daba lugar el maltratamiento que el mal ciego dende allí adelante me hacía, que sin causa ni razón me hería, dándome coscorrones y repelándome. Y si alguno le decía por qué me trataba tan mal, luego contaba el cuento del jarro, diciendo: —¿Pensaréis que este mi mozo es algún inocente? Pues oíd si el demonio ensayara otra tal hazaña.

Santiguándose los que lo oían, decían: —¡Mirá quién pensara de un muchacho tan pequeño tal ruindad!

Y reían mucho el artificio, y decíanle: —Castigaldo, castigaldo, que de Dios lo habréis.

Y él, con aquello, nunca otra cosa hacía.

Y en esto, yo siempre le llevaba por los peores caminos, y adrede, por le hacer mal y daño; si había piedras, por ellas; si lodo, por lo más alto, que aunque yo no iba por lo más enjuto, holgábame a mí de quebrar un ojo por quebrar dos al que ninguno tenía. Con esto siempre con el cabo alto del tiento me

turned skyward and my eyes slightly closed to heighten my pleasure in the tasty liquid, the frenzied blind man sensed that it was the right moment to avenge himself on me; with all his strength he raised that sweet and bitter jug with both hands and brought it down on my mouth, using maximum force, as I said; so that I, poor Lázaro, suspecting nothing and carefree and happy as in the past, really thought that the sky and everything in it had tumbled down on me.

The little love tap was so hard that it stunned me and knocked me out; the blow with the jug was so strong that the flying pieces dug into my face, cutting it in many places, and broke my teeth, which have been missing to this very day. From that time on, I disliked the nasty blind man; and, even though he liked me, nourished me, and looked after me, I saw all too well that he had been amused by that cruel punishment. He washed out with wine the cuts that the jar fragments had made, and said with a smile:

"What do you think, Lázaro? The same thing that made you ill is curing you and restoring your health." And other jokes that I didn't find funny.

Once I was half-cured of my rotten punishment[23] and bruises, I reflected that with a few more such blows the cruel blind man could get rid of me, and I determined to get rid of *him*; but I didn't do so right away, in order to do it with less harm and more advantage to myself. Even though I wanted to calm down my heart and forgive him for the blow with the jug, I was prevented from doing so by the bad way in which the nasty blind man treated me from that time on; he would hurt me for no reason at all, thumping me on the head and pulling out my hair. If anyone asked him why he was mistreating me that way, he would immediately tell them the story of the jug, saying: "You probably think that this boy of mine is some little innocent. Well, listen and then tell me whether the Devil himself would attempt a deed like this one."

The listeners would cross themselves and say: "Just look! Who'd have thought such a little boy could be so evil!"

And they had a good laugh over the trick, and they told him: "Punish him, punish him, and God will reward you for it."

Hearing that, he never did anything else.

Meanwhile, I always led him over the roughest paths, on purpose, to do him harm and hurt; if there were stones, over them; if there was mud, through the thickest of it, because, even though I myself wasn't walking through the driest spots, I was pleased to put out one of my own eyes in order to put out both of his—and he hadn't any. At the

---

23. A word play: *negra trepa* can also mean "a black edging" (his bruises).

atentaba el colodrillo, el cual siempre traía lleno de tolondrones y pelado de sus manos; y aunque yo juraba no lo hacer con malicia, sino por no hallar mejor camino, no me aprovechaba ni me creía, mas tal era el sentido y el grandísimo entendimiento del traidor.

Y porque vea Vuestra Merced a cuánto se extendía el ingenio deste astuto ciego, contaré un caso de muchos que con él me acaecieron, en el cual me parece dio bien a entender su gran astucia. Cuando salimos de Salamanca, su motivo fue venir a tierra de Toledo, porque decía ser la gente más rica, aunque no muy limosnera; arrimábase a este refrán: "Más da el duro que el desnudo." Y venimos a este camino por los mejores lugares. Donde hallaba buena acogida y ganancia, deteníamonos; donde no, a tercero día hacíamos San Juan.

Acaeció que, llegando a un lugar que llaman Almorox al tiempo que cogían las uvas, un vendimiador le dio un racimo dellas en limosna. Y como suelen ir los cestos maltratados, y también porque la uva en aquel tiempo está muy madura, desgranábasele el racimo en la mano; para echarlo en el fardel, tornábase mosto y lo que a él se llegaba. Acordó de hacer un banquete, ansí por no lo poder llevar como por contentarme que aquel día me había dado muchos rodillazos y golpes. Sentámonos en un valladar, y dijo:

—Agora quiero yo usar contigo de una liberalidad, y es que ambos comamos este racimo de uvas, y que hayas dél tanta parte como yo. Partillo hemos desta manera: tú picarás una vez, y yo otra; con tal que me prometas no tomar cada vez más de una uva. Yo haré lo mesmo hasta que lo acabemos, y desta suerte no habrá engaño.

Hecho ansí el concierto, comenzamos; mas luego al segundo lance, el traidor mudó propósito, y comenzó a tomar de dos en dos, considerando que yo debría hacer lo mismo. Como vi que él quebraba la postura, no me contenté ir a la par con él, mas aún pasaba adelante: dos a dos, y tres a tres, y como podía, las comía. Acabado el racimo, estuvo un poco con el escobajo en la mano, y meneando la cabeza dijo:

—Lázaro, engañado me has; juraré yo a Dios que has comido las uvas tres a tres.

same time, he constantly poked the back of my neck with the raised end of his cane, and my neck was always full of bumps and plucked by his hands. Even though I swore I wasn't leading him astray maliciously, but couldn't find any better path, that did me no good; he didn't believe me, such was the villain's good sense and great intelligence.

So that Your Honor may see how far this shrewd blind man's cleverness went, I'll narrate one incident among many that I experienced with him, one in which I think he exhibited his great shrewdness clearly. When we left Salamanca, his intention was to head for Toledo territory, because he said the people there had more money, even though they weren't very charitable. He used to cite the proverb: "The hard-hearted man gives more than the destitute one." And we stopped at the best places along that road. Wherever he found a good reception and income, we would linger; otherwise, we would make tracks on the third day.

It happened that, arriving in a town called Almorox[24] at the time of the grape harvest, a vintager gave him a bunch of grapes as alms. Since the baskets are usually roughly handled, and also because the grapes were very ripe at the time, the grapes came right off the stalk in one's hand. If the bunch had been placed in the sack, it would have turned to juice and ruined everything else in there. He decided to make a feast, because he couldn't keep it, and to give me a little pleasure, since on that day he had given me numerous blows with his knees and with his hands. We sat down against a fence, and he said:

"Now I want to be generous to you, like this: Let's both eat this bunch of grapes, with you and me having equal shares. We'll divide it this way: You'll take one bite, then I will, but you must promise me not to eat more than one grape at a time. I'll do the same until we finish, and that way no one will be cheated."

After making that arrangement, we began; but as early as the second round, the villain changed his mind and started eating two at a time, feeling sure that I was doing the same. When I saw that he was breaking our agreement, I wasn't satisfied with keeping up with him, but I even outdid him: I ate them two at a time, three at a time, and any way I could. When the bunch was finished, he remained a while with the bare stalk in his hand, then said, shaking his head:

"Lázaro, you've cheated me; I'll swear to God that you ate the grapes three at a time."

---

24. All the places between Salamanca and Toledo mentioned in this chapter and the next are real, and really so situated.

—No comí — dije yo—, mas ¿por qué sospecháis eso?

Respondió el sagacísimo ciego: —¿Sabes en qué veo que las comiste tres a tres? En que comía yo dos a dos y callabas.

[A lo cual yo no respondí. Yendo que íbamos ansí por debajo de unos soportales, en Escalona, adonde a la sazón estábamos, en casa de un zapatero había muchas sogas y otras cosas que de esparto se hacen, y parte dellas dieron a mi amo en la cabeza; el cual alzando la mano tocó en ellas, y viendo lo que era díjome:

—Anda presto, mochacho, salgamos de entre tan mal manjar, que ahoga sin comerlo.

Yo que bien descuidado iba de aquello, miré lo que era, y como no vi sino sogas y cinchas, que no era cosa de comer, díjele: —Tío, ¿por qué decís eso?

Respondióme: —Calla, sobrino, según las mañas que llevas, lo sabrás, y verás cómo digo verdad.

Y ansí pasamos adelante por el mismo portal, y llegamos a un mesón, a la puerta del cual había muchos cuernos en la pared, donde ataban los recueros sus bestias, y como iba tentando si era allí el mesón adonde él rezaba cada día por la mesonera la oración de la emparedada, asió de un cuerno, y con un gran sospiro, dijo:

—¡Oh mala cosa, peor que tienes la hechura! ¡De cuántos eres deseado poner tu nombre sobre cabeza ajena, y de cuán pocos tenerte, ni aun oír nombre por ninguna vía!

Como le oí lo que decía, dije: —Tío, ¿qué es esto que decís?

—Calla, sobrino, que algún día te dará éste que en la mano tengo alguna mala comida y cena.

—No le comeré yo —dije—, y no me la dará.

—Yo te digo verdad; si no, verlo has, si vives.

Y ansí pasamos adelante, hasta la puerta del mesón, adonde pluguiere a Dios nunca allá llegáramos, según lo que me sucedía en él.

Era todo lo más que rezaba por mesoneras, y por bodegoneras y turroneras y rameras, y ansí por semejantes mujercillas, que por hombre casi nunca le vi decir oración.]

Reíme entre mí, y aunque mochacho, noté mucho la discreta consideración del ciego.

"I didn't," I said, "but why do you have that suspicion?"

The immensely wise blind man replied: "Do you know how I can tell that you ate them three at a time? Because I was eating them two at a time, and you didn't say anything."[25]

[To which I made no reply. As we were thus walking beneath some arcades in Escalona, where we were at the time, there were hanging outside a shoemaker's shop many ropes and other things made of esparto grass. Some of them grazed my master's head; raising his hand, he touched them and, recognizing what they were, he said:

"Walk fast, boy, let's not remain amid such bad food, which chokes you even if you don't eat it."

I, who hadn't been paying any attention to that stuff, looked to see what it was, and, seeing nothing but ropes and girths, which weren't edible, I said: "'Uncle,' why do you say that?"

He replied: "Quiet, 'nephew.' To judge by the tricks you play, you'll find out what I mean, and you'll learn I'm telling the truth."

And so we kept walking along the same arcade, and we arrived at an inn, by the door of which many horns were fastened to the wall, for the horse and mule drovers to tie up their animals. As he groped around to learn whether that was the inn where he recited the "prayer of the immured woman"[26] every day for the innkeeper's wife, he took hold of a horn and, sighing deeply, said:

"Oh, you evil thing, even worse than your shape! How many men want to see your name attached to other men's heads, and how few want to possess you or even hear you mentioned in any way!"

When I heard him say that, I said: "'Uncle,' what do you mean?"

"Quiet, 'nephew'; one day what I'm holding in my hand will give you an unpleasant meal and supper."

"I won't eat it," I said, "so it won't."

"I'm telling you the truth; if not, you'll find out, if you live."

And so we walked onward, up to the door of the inn, and I wish to God we had never arrived there, because of what happened to me there.

Most of his prayers were for innkeepers' wives, tavernkeepers' wives, nougat-makers' wives, prostitutes, and suchlike no-account women; I hardly ever saw him reciting prayers for men.]

I laughed to myself and, though still a boy, I took careful note of the blind man's subtle reasoning.

---

25. The following passage enclosed in square brackets is an interpolation found only in the Alcalá edition (of the three 1554 editions; see Introduction).   26. One of the stock charms for restoring health in the repertoire of blind beggars.

Mas por no ser prolijo, dejo de contar muchas cosas, así graciosas como de notar, que con este mi primer amo me acaecieron, y quiero decir el despidiente y, con él, acabar. Estábamos en Escalona, villa del duque della, en un mesón, y diome un pedazo de longaniza que le asase. Ya que la longaniza había pringado y comídose las pringadas, sacó un maravedí de la bolsa y mandó que fuese por él de vino a la taberna. Púsome el demonio el aparejo delante los ojos, el cual, como suelen decir, hace al ladrón, y fue que había cabe el fuego un nabo pequeño, larguillo y ruinoso y tal, que por no ser para la olla, debió ser echado allí.

Y como al presente nadie estuviese sino él y yo solos, como me vi con apetito goloso, habiéndome puesto dentro el sabroso olor de la longaniza (del cual solamente sabía que había de gozar), no mirando qué me podría suceder, pospuesto todo el temor por cumplir con el deseo, en tanto que el ciego sacaba de la bolsa el dinero, saqué la longaniza, y, muy presto, metí el sobredicho nabo en el asador, el cual, mi amo dándome el dinero para el vino, tomó y comenzó a dar vueltas al fuego, queriendo asar al que de ser cocido, por sus deméritos, había escapado.

Yo fui por el vino, con el cual no tardé en despachar la longaniza; y cuando vine, hallé al pecador del ciego que tenía entre dos rebanadas apretado el nabo, al cual aún no había conocido por no lo haber tentado con la mano. Como tomase las rebanadas y mordiese en ellas, pensando también llevar parte de la longaniza, hallóse en frío con el frío nabo; alteróse y dijo: —¿Qué es esto, Lazarillo?

—¡Lacerado de mí! —dije yo—. ¿Si queréis a mí echar algo? ¿Yo no vengo de traer el vino? Alguno estaba ahí, y por burlar haría esto.

—No, no —dijo él—, que yo no he dejado el asador de la mano. No es posible.

Yo torné a jurar y perjurar que estaba libre de aquel trueco y cambio; mas poco me aprovechó, pues a las astucias del maldito ciego nada se le escondía. Levantóse y asióme por la cabeza y llegóse a olerme. Y como debió sentir el huelgo, a uso de buen podenco, por mejor satisfacerse de la verdad y con la gran agonía que llevaba, asiéndome con las manos, abríame la boca

But, so as not to go on too long, I omit the narration of many incidents, both humorous and noteworthy, that I experienced with this first master of mine, and I'll go on to tell about our parting of the ways, and thus bring this section of my story to a close. We were in Escalona, a town in the possession of a duke, and we were staying at an inn, when he gave me a piece of sausage to roast for him. After the grease had oozed from the sausage and we had eaten bread smeared with the grease, he took a *maravedí* out of his purse and sent me to buy wine with it at the tavern. The Devil showed me the opportunity, which makes the thief, as the saying goes, and it was this: Near the fire was a small turnip, longish and damaged, so that it must have been thrown there as being no good for the stewpot.

Since at the moment no one was there but the two of us, and since I found myself leaning toward the sin of gluttony, having inhaled the delicious aroma of the sausage (and knowing that that was all I was going to enjoy of it), I paid no heed to what might befall me and I set aside all my fears in order to achieve my desire. While the blind man was taking the money out of his purse, I removed the sausage and very speedily put the above-mentioned turnip on the spit. After giving me the money for the wine, my master took the spit and started turning it over the fire, wishing to roast something that had escaped being boiled on account of its defects.

I went for the wine, and after I got it, it didn't take me long to polish off the sausage. When I returned I found the blind sinner holding the turnip pressed between two slices of bread; he hadn't recognized it because he hadn't touched it with his hands. When he took the sandwich and bit into it, thinking he was also getting some of the sausage, he remained dumbfounded with that dumb turnip. He got upset and said: "What's this, Lazarillo?"

"Woe is me!"[27] I said. "Are you actually trying to blame me? Didn't I just get back with the wine? Someone must have been here who did this as a joke."

"No, no," he said, "because I never let the spit out of my hand. It's impossible."

I continued to swear up and down that I was innocent of that swap and exchange; but it did me little good, because nothing could be concealed from that damned blind man's cunning. He got up and grabbed me by the head and came up close, in order to smell me. And since he must have smelled my breath, like a good hunting dog, in order to get closer to the truth and because he was suffering such great anxiety, he

---

27. The Spanish has a pun on *Lazarillo* and *lacerado*.

más de su derecho y desatentadamente metía la nariz, la cual él tenía luenga y afilada, y a aquella sazón, con el enojo, se había augmentado un palmo, con el pico de la cual me llegó a la gulilla.

Y con esto, y con el gran miedo que tenía, y con la brevedad del tiempo, la negra longaniza aún no había hecho asiento en el estómago, y lo más principal, con el destiento de la cumplidísima nariz medio cuasi ahogándome, todas estas cosas se juntaron, y fueron causa que el hecho y golosina se manifestase y lo suyo fuese vuelto a su dueño; de manera que antes que el mal ciego sacase de mi boca su trompa, tal alteración sintió mi estómago, que le dio con el hurto en ella, de suerte que su nariz y la negra mal mascada longaniza a un tiempo salieron de mi boca.

¡Oh gran Dios, quién estuviera aquella hora sepultado, que muerto ya lo estaba! Fue tal el coraje del perverso ciego, que, si al ruido no acudieran, pienso no me dejara con la vida. Sacáronme de entre sus manos, dejándoselas llenas de aquellos pocos cabellos que tenía, arañada la cara y rascuñado el pescuezo y la garganta. Y esto bien lo merecía, pues por su maldad me venían tantas persecuciones.

Contaba el mal ciego a todos cuantos allí se allegaban mis desastres, y dábales cuenta una y otra vez, así de la del jarro como de la del racimo, y agora de lo presente. Era la risa de todos tan grande, que toda la gente que por la calle pasaba entraba a ver la fiesta; mas con tanta gracia y donaire recontaba el ciego mis hazañas, que aunque yo estaba tan maltratado y llorando, me parecía que hacía sinjusticia en no se las reír.

Y en cuanto esto pasaba, a la memoria me vino una cobardía y flojedad que hice por que me maldecía, y fue no dejalle sin narices, pues tan buen tiempo tuve para ello, que la mitad del camino estaba andado: que, con sólo apretar los dientes, se me quedaran en casa, y con ser de aquel malvado, por ventura lo retuviera mejor mi estómago que retuyo la longaniza, y no pareciendo ellas pudiera negar la demanda.

grabbed me with his hands, opened my mouth much too wide, and carelessly thrust in his nose, which was long and sharp and which his vexation had made a span longer at the moment, so that its tip reached to my epiglottis.

Because of this and because of my great fear and the shortness of the time that had elapsed, the damned sausage had not yet settled in my stomach. Most of all, I was half-choking because of the lack of moderation of that most abundant nose.[28] All of these things combined, and brought it about that my deed and my greed became clear, and everything was returned to its lawful owner: because, before the nasty blind man removed his snout from my mouth, my stomach became so queasy that the stolen goods assailed it, so that his nose and the damned, badly chewed sausage came out of my mouth at one and the same time.

Oh, great God, how I wished I were already buried at that moment, because I was definitely already a dead man! The evil blind man's anger was so great that, if people hadn't come running when they heard the racket, I don't think he would have spared my life. I was wrenched out of his hands, which remained full of those few hairs I still had on my head; my face was scratched, and my neck and throat all torn up. And my throat deserved it, because it was for its wickedness that I had received such a great punishment.

The nasty blind man kept recounting my misfortunes to everyone who arrived there, and he repeatedly informed them of my ruse with the jug, the one with the grapes, and this current one. Everyone laughed so loud that all the people passing by on the street came in to view the celebration; but the blind man went on recounting my exploits with such humor and wit that, even though I was so manhandled, and weeping over it, I felt I was being unjust not to laugh over them.

While this was going on, it occurred to me that I had been cowardly and weak, and I cursed myself for it. Why hadn't I left him without a nose, since I had had such a good opportunity to do so, seeing it had already gone halfway? Merely by bearing down with my teeth,[29] I would have kept it with me, and, even though it belonged to that villain, my stomach might have kept it down better than the sausage; since the nose would no longer have been visible as evidence, I could

---

28. Or: "the discourtesy of that very polite nose." Other translations, such as "disturbance" and "excess," have been suggested for the very rare word *destiento*. 29. Lázaro was most likely exaggerating earlier when he said that the blow with the jug knocked out his teeth, or else he meant only a few teeth, because he makes much use of his dentition in the rest of the novel.

Pluguiera a Dios que lo hubiera hecho, que eso fuera así que así.

Hiciéronnos amigos la mesonera y los que allí estaban, y con el vino que para beber le había traído laváronme la cara y la garganta. Sobre lo cual discantaba el mal ciego donaires, diciendo:

—Por verdad, más vino me gasta este mozo en lavatorios al cabo del año que yo bebo en dos. A lo menos, Lázaro, eres en más cargo al vino que a tu padre, porque él una vez te engendró, mas el vino mil te ha dado la vida.

Y luego contaba cuántas veces me había descalabrado y arpado la cara, y con vino luego sanaba.

—Yo te digo —dijo— que si un hombre en el mundo ha de ser bienaventurado con vino, que serás tú.

Y reían mucho, los que me lavaban, con esto, aunque yo renegaba. Mas el pronóstico del ciego no salió mentiroso, y después acá muchas veces me acuerdo de aquel hombre, que sin duda debía tener espíritu de profecía, y me pesa de los sinsabores que le hice, aunque bien se lo pagué, considerando lo que aquel día me dijo salirme tan verdadero como adelante Vuestra Merced oirá.

Visto esto y las malas burlas que el ciego burlaba de mí, determiné de todo en todo dejalle, y como lo traía pensado y lo tenía en voluntad, con este postrer juego que me hizo, afirmélo más. Y fue ansí, que luego otro día salimos por la villa a pedir limosna y había llovido mucho la noche antes; y porque el día también llovía, y andaba rezando debajo de unos portales que en aquel pueblo había, donde no nos mojamos; mas como la noche se venía, y el llover no cesaba, díjome el ciego: —Lázaro, esta agua es muy porfiada, y cuanto la noche más cierra, más recia; acojámonos a la posada con tiempo.

Para ir allá, habíamos de pasar un arroyo que con la mucha agua iba grande. Yo le dije: —Tío, el arroyo va muy ancho; mas si queréis, yo veo por donde travesemos más aína sin nos mojar, porque se estrecha allí mucho, y saltando pasaremos a pie enjuto.

Parecióle buen consejo, y dijo: —Discreto eres, por esto te quiero bien. Llévame a ese lugar donde el arroyo se ensangosta,

have denied any accusation. I wish to God I had done it, because it wouldn't have made any difference in my situation.[30]

We were reconciled by the innkeeper's wife and the bystanders, and with the wine I had brought him to drink they washed my face and throat. The nasty blind man supplied a counterpoint of jokes to this operation, saying:

"To tell the truth, I use more wine each year in washing this boy than I drink in two. At any rate, Lázaro, you owe more to wine than you do to your father, because he begot you only once, but the wine has given you life a thousand times."

And then he told them how often he had injured my head and lacerated my face, which he would then heal with wine.

"I tell you," he said to me, "that if anyone in the world is destined to have luck with wine, it's you."

And those who were washing me had a good laugh at that, even though I protested. But the blind man's prediction wasn't false, and since then I have frequently recalled that man, who must surely have had the spirit of prophecy, and I feel sorry for the troubles I caused him, although I paid dearly for them, when I reflect on the accuracy of what he told me that day, as Your Honor will hear later on.

Considering this and the nasty tricks the blind man played on me, I decided definitely to leave him; it had been on my mind and in my wishes, and after this last game he played with me, I became more determined. And so, the very next day we set out to beg alms in town; it had rained hard the night before, and, since it was raining during the day as well, he was walking along reciting prayers beneath certain arcades located in that town, where we didn't get wet. But when night was approaching and the rain didn't stop, the blind man said to me: "Lázaro, this rain shows no sign of letting up, and it gets stronger the closer we get to nighttime; let's take shelter in the inn while we have time."

To get there we had to pass a stream that was swollen with the heavy rain. I said: "'Uncle,' the stream is very wide; but, if you like, I see a place where we can cross it more quickly without getting wet, because it becomes very narrow there and we can avoid wetting our feet if we jump over it."

It sounded like good advice to him, and he said: "You're thoughtful, and that's why I like you. Take me to that spot where the stream

---

30. Numerous other translations have been suggested for the uncommon expression *así que así*.

que agora es invierno y sabe mal el agua, y más llevar los pies mojados.

Yo, que vi el aparejo a mi deseo, saquéle de bajo de los portales, y llevéle derecho a un pilar o poste de piedra que en la plaza estaba, sobre el cual y sobre otros cargaban saledizos de aquellas casas, y dígole: —Tío, éste es el paso más angosto que en el arroyo hay.

Como llovía recio y el triste se mojaba, y con la priesa que llevábamos de salir del agua, que encima de nos caía, y lo más principal, porque Dios le cegó aquella hora el entendimiento (fue por darme dél venganza), creyóse de mí y dijo: —Ponme bien derecho y salta tú el arroyo.

Yo le puse bien derecho enfrente del pilar, y doy un salto y póngome detrás del poste como quien espera tope de toro y díjele: —¡Sús! Saltá todo lo que podáis, porque deis deste cabo del agua.

Aun apenas lo había acabado de decir, cuando se abalanza el pobre ciego como cabrón, y de toda su fuerza arremete, tomando un paso atrás de la corrida para hacer mayor salto, y da con la cabeza en el poste, que sonó tan recio como si diera con una gran calabaza, y cayó luego para atrás, medio muerto y hendida la cabeza.

—¿Cómo, y olistes la longaniza y no el poste? ¡Olé! ¡Olé! —le dije yo.

Y dejéle en poder de mucha gente que lo había ido a socorrer, y tomé la puerta de la villa en los pies de un trote, y antes que la noche viniese di comigo en Torrijos. No supe más lo que Dios dél hizo, ni curé de lo saber.

## TRATADO SEGUNDO

### Cómo Lázaro se asentó con un clérigo y de las cosas que con él pasó

Otro día, no pareciéndome estar allí seguro, fuime a un lugar que llaman Maqueda, adonde me toparon mis pecados con un clérigo, que llegando a pedir limosna, me preguntó si sabía ayudar a misa. Yo dije que sí, como era verdad, que aunque maltratado, mil cosas buenas me mostró el pecador del ciego, y una dellas fue ésta. Finalmente el clérigo me recibió por suyo.

narrows, because it's wintertime and the water isn't attractive, especially when you get your feet wet."

Seeing the opportune nature of the situation, I led him out from under the arcade and brought him straight to a stone pillar or post that stood in the square, one of those on which the overhangs of the houses rested, and I said: "'Uncle,' this is the narrowest spot in the whole stream."

Since it was raining hard and the miserable man was getting wet, and since we were in a hurry to get out of the water that was falling on us, but especially because God blinded his intelligence at that moment, in order to avenge me for what he had done to me, he believed me, and said: "Point me in the right direction, and then jump over the stream yourself."

I placed him directly in front of the post, gave a jump, and hid behind the post like a man awaiting a bull's head-butt. Then I said: "Come on! Jump as hard as you can, to get on this side of the stream."

I had scarcely finished saying this when the poor blind man hurled himself forward like a billy-goat, charging with all his might and taking a step backward from his course in order to jump higher. He rammed his head against the post, which made a sound as loud as if it had been struck by a big pumpkin. He immediately fell backward, half dead, with his head split open.

"What? You smelled the sausage and not the post? Smell! Smell!" I said to him.

And I left him in the hands of a number of people who had run up to help him. I dashed out of the town gate at a trot, and before nightfall I reached Torrijos. I never found out what God had done with him, nor was I interested in finding out.

## CHAPTER TWO

## How Lázaro Was Employed by a Priest, and of the Things That Befell Him in His Company

The next day, not considering myself safe there, I went to a town called Maqueda, where, to pay for my sins, I came across a priest who, when I went up to him to beg for alms, asked me if I knew how to serve as an altar boy. I said yes, which was true, because, even though he mistreated me, that blind sinner had taught me a thousand useful things, and this was one. Finally the priest took me into his service.

Escapé del trueno y di en el relámpago, porque era el ciego para con éste un Alejandre Magno, con ser la mesma avaricia, como he contado. No digo más sino que toda la laceria del mundo estaba encerrada en éste (no sé si de su cosecha era o lo había anexado con el hábito de clerecía).

Él tenía un arcaz viejo y cerrado con su llave, la cual traía atada con una agujeta del paletoque, y en viniendo el bodigo de la iglesia, por su mano era luego allí lanzado, y tornada a cerrar el arca; y en toda la casa no había ninguna cosa de comer, como suele estar en otras: algún tocino colgado al humero, algún queso puesto en alguna tabla o en el armario, algún canastillo con algunos pedazos de pan que de la mesa sobran, que me parece a mí que aunque dello no me aprovechara, con la vista dello me consolara.

Solamente había una horca de cebollas, y tras la llave, en una cámara en lo alto de la casa. Déstas tenía yo de ración una para cada cuatro días, y cuando le pedía la llave para ir por ella, si alguno estaba presente, echaba mano al falsopeto, y, con gran continencia, la desataba y me la daba, diciendo: —Toma, y vuélvela luego, y no hagáis sino golosinar.

Como si debajo della estuvieran todas las conservas de Valencia, con no haber en la dicha cámara, como dije, maldita la otra cosa que las cebollas colgadas de un clavo, las cuales él tenía tan bien por cuenta, que si por malos de mis pecados me desmandara a más de mi tasa, me costara caro. Finalmente, yo me finaba de hambre.

Pues ya que comigo tenía poca caridad, consigo usaba más. Cinco blancas de carne era su ordinario para comer y cenar. Verdad es que partía comigo del caldo. Que de la carne, ¡tan blanco el ojo!, sino un poco de pan, y ¡pluguiera a Dios que me demediara!

Los sábados cómense en esta tierra cabezas de carnero, y enviábame por una que costaba tres maravedís. Aquélla le cocía y comía los ojos, y la lengua, y el cogote y sesos, y la carne que en las quijadas tenía, y dábame todos los huesos roídos, y dábamelos en el plato, diciendo: —Toma, come, triunfa, que para ti es el mundo: ¡mejor vida tienes que el Papa!

"¡Tal te la dé Dios!", decía yo paso entre mí.

A cabo de tres semanas que estuve con él, vine a tanta

I had escaped from the frying pan into the fire,[31] because in comparison with this priest, the blind man was as generous as Alexander the Great, even though he was the embodiment of miserliness, as I've told you. I merely state that all the stinginess in the world was contained in this priest, whether it was inborn in him or he had acquired it along with his clerical cloth.

He possessed an old strongbox, locked with a key that he wore tied to his scapular-like cape with a metal-tipped belt. When the rich loaves of bread that had been offered in church for his use were brought to the house, he immediately put them in that box personally and locked the box again. Nowhere in the house was there anything to eat, as there generally is in others: some bacon hanging in the fireplace hood, some cheese lying on a shelf or in the cupboard, some basket with a few pieces of bread left over from the table. It seems to me that, even if I didn't have access to them, the sight of them would have consoled me.

There was merely a string of onions, and that locked away, too, in a room on the top floor. My ration was one of these every four days; when I asked him for the key to go get one, if someone else was present he would lay hold of the purse that hung on his breast and, very gravely, would take out the key and give it to me, saying: "Here, but come right back and don't hang around snacking."

As if that room contained all the fruit preserves of Valencia, although, as I said, there wasn't a single thing in it but the onions hanging on a nail! And he kept such a careful count of them that if, for my deadly sins, I had recklessly helped myself to more than my normal portion, it would have cost me dear. In short, my life was being cut short by hunger.

But if he showed me scant charity, he showed himself more. His daily ration for dinner and supper was five *blancas'* worth of meat. True, he shared the broth with me. As for the meat, out of the question! I got just a little bread, and I wish to God it had been even half of what I needed!

In that region people eat sheeps' heads on Saturdays, and he used to send me for one that cost three *maravedís*. He would boil it and eat the eyes, tongue, neck, brains, and the meat clinging to the jawbones. He would give me all the bones after he had gnawed them, handing them to me on the platter with the words: "Here, eat and rejoice, because the world is yours: you're better off than the Pope!"

"God give you such a life!" I would say quietly to myself.

At the end of three weeks with him, I had become so thin that my

---

31. Literally: "from the thunder into the lightning."

flaqueza, que no me podía tener en las piernas de pura hambre. Vime claramente ir a la sepultura, si Dios y mi saber no me remediaran. Para usar de mis mañas no tenía aparejo, por no tener en qué dalle salto, y aunque algo hubiera, no podía cegalle, como hacía al que Dios perdone (si de aquella calabazada feneció), que todavía, aunque astuto, con faltalle aquel preciado sentido, no me sentía, mas estotro, ninguno hay que tan aguda vista tuviese como él tenía.

Cuando al ofertorio estábamos, ninguna blanca en la concha caía que no era dél registrada: el un ojo tenía en la gente y el otro en mis manos. Bailábanle los ojos en el casco como si fueran de azogue. Cuantas blancas ofrecían tenía por cuenta, y acabado el ofrecer, luego me quitaba la corneta y la ponía sobre el altar.

No era yo señor de asirle una blanca todo el tiempo que con él viví, o, por mejor decir, morí. De la taberna nunca le traje una blanca de vino, mas aquel poco que de la ofrenda había metido en su arcaz, compasaba de tal forma, que le turaba toda la semana. Y por ocultar su gran mezquindad, decíame: —Mira, mozo, los sacerdotes han de ser muy templados en su comer y beber, y por esto yo no me desmando como otros. —Mas el lacerado mentía falsamente, porque en cofradías y mortuorios que rezamos, a costa ajena comía como lobo, y bebía más que un saludador.

Y porque dije de mortuorios, Dios me perdone que jamás fui enemigo de la naturaleza humana, sino entonces; y esto era porque comíamos bien y me hartaban. Deseaba y aún rogaba a Dios que cada día matase el suyo. Y cuando dábamos sacramento a los enfermos, especialmente la Extremaunción, como manda el clérigo rezar a los que están allí, yo cierto no era el postrero de la oración, y con todo mi corazón y buena voluntad rogaba al Señor, no que la echase a la parte que más servido fuese, como se suele decir, mas que le llevase de aqueste mundo. Y cuando alguno de éstos escapaba (Dios me lo perdone), que mil veces le daba al diablo, y el que se moría, otras tantas bendiciones llevaba de mí dichas. Porque en todo el tiempo que allí estuve, que sería cuasi seis meses, solas veinte

legs wouldn't hold me up, I was so hungry. I saw myself clearly headed for the grave, unless God and my brains helped me out. I had no opportunity to employ my ruses, because there was nothing to steal; even if there had been, I couldn't put blinders on him, as I did with my first master (may God forgive him, if he died of that knock on the head), who after all, though he was so clever, couldn't see me because he lacked that precious sense. But as for this new master, no one was as sharp-sighted as he was.

When we were collecting money in church, no *blanca* fell into the plate[32] that he didn't register: he kept one eye on the people and the other on my hands. His eyes danced around in his skull as if they were quicksilver. He kept count of every *blanca* in the offering, and when the offering was over, he immediately took the plate away from me and placed it on the altar.

I wasn't able to get hold of a *blanca* the whole time that I lived with him, or died with him, to be more exact. I never brought him a *blanca*'s worth of wine from the tavern; instead, he measured out the little that he received at the offering so carefully that it lasted him all week. To conceal his enormous stinginess, he used to say to me: "You see, boy, priests have to be very moderate in eating and drinking, and that's why I don't indulge myself like other people." But the wretch was lying in his teeth, because at the meetings of religious societies and at the funerals where we prayed, if someone else was paying, he used to eat like a wolf and drink more than a faith healer.[33]

And since I have mentioned funerals, may God forgive me, because I've never been an enemy of the human race except at that time; and this was because we ate well and I got filled up. I used to wish, and even pray to God, that someone would die every day. And when we gave sacraments to the sick, especially Extreme Unction, when the priest orders everyone present to pray, I was definitely not the last to join in the prayer. With all my heart and will I prayed the Lord, not to take notice of the prayer in the way that best suited His purposes, but to remove the sick person from this world. And when one of them recovered (God forgive me), I wished a thousand times that the Devil would take him. Anyone who died received that same number of blessings from me. Because in the whole time I remained there, which would be nearly six months, only twenty people died, and I'm

---

32. Literally: "shell." The word for "plate" later in this paragraph seems to mean a clerical cap, but *corneta* may be a typographical error for *concheta* ("little shell").    33. Faith healers apparently drank a lot because they used a lot of their own saliva in their cures.

personas fallecieron, y éstas bien creo que las maté yo, o, por mejor decir, murieron a mi recuesta. Porque viendo el Señor mi rabiosa y continua muerte, pienso que holgaba de matarlos por darme a mí vida.

Mas de lo que al presente padecía remedio no hallaba; que si el día que enterrábamos yo vivía, los días que no había muerto, por quedar bien vezado de la hartura, tornando a mi cuotidiana hambre, más lo sentía. De manera que en nada hallaba descanso, salvo en la muerte, que yo también para mí como para los otros, deseaba algunas veces; mas no la vía, aunque estaba siempre en mí.

Pensé muchas veces irme de aquel mezquino amo, mas por dos cosas lo dejaba: la primera, por no me atrever a mis piernas, por temer de la flaqueza, que de pura hambre me venía; y la otra, consideraba y decía: "Yo he tenido dos amos: el primero traíame muerto de hambre, y dejándole, topé con estotro, que me tiene ya con ella en la sepultura; pues si deste desisto y doy en otro más bajo, ¿qué será sino fenecer?" Con esto no me osaba menear, porque tenía por fe que todos los grados había de hallar más ruines. Y a abajar otro punto, no sonara Lázaro ni se oyera en el mundo.

Pues estando en tal aflición (cual plega al Señor librar della a todo fiel cristiano), y sin saber darme consejo, viéndome ir de mal en peor, un día que el cuitado, ruin y lacerado de mi amo había ido fuera del lugar, llegóse acaso a mi puerta un calderero, el cual yo creo que fue ángel enviado a mí por la mano de Dios en aquel hábito. Preguntóme si tenía algo que adobar. "En mí teníades bien que hacer, y no haríades poco si me remediásedes", dije paso, que no me oyó.

Mas como no era tiempo de gastarlo en decir gracias, alumbrado por el Espíritu Santo, le dije: —Tío, una llave de este arte he perdido, y temo mi señor me azote. Por vuestra vida, veáis si en ésas que traéis hay alguna que le haga, que yo os lo pagaré.

Comenzó a probar el angélico calderero una y otra de un gran sartal que dellas traía, y yo a ayudalle con mis flacas oraciones. Cuando no me cato, veo en figura de panes, como dicen, la cara de Dios dentro del arcaz, y abierto, díjele: —Yo no tengo dineros que os dar por la llave, mas tomad de ahí el pago.

sure that I was the one who killed them—or, to be more exact, that they died at my request. Because I think that when the Lord saw how ravenously hungry I always was, He was pleased to kill them to give life to me.

But I was unable to find any remedy for my suffering at that time, because, if I lived on days when we buried someone, on days without a victim, since I had grown accustomed to filling my belly, I felt my daily hunger all the more when I returned to it. So that I saw no possible relief except in death, which I sometimes wished for myself as well as for others; but I couldn't find it, even though it was always inside me.

Often I thought about abandoning that stingy master, but I refrained for two reasons. The first was that I didn't trust my legs for fear of the weakness that came from hunger alone. The second was that I reflected: "I've had two masters: the first one kept me dead of hunger, and, when I left him, I ran across this one, who has nearly brought me to my grave with it. Now, if I leave this one and wind up with one of lower quality, what will it mean but my doom?" And so I didn't dare make a move, because I was convinced that every step would lead downward to something worse. And if I moved just a jot lower, the name of Lázaro would be buried in silence, never again to be heard in the world.

Well, while I was in this distress (from which may the Lord deliver all faithful Christians) and unable to work out any plan, seeing myself go from bad to worse, one day, when that unhappy, evil, wretched master of mine had gone out of town, by chance there came to my door a tinker, who I think was an angel sent to me by the hand of God in that guise. He asked me if I had anything to mend. "You'd find plenty to do if you wanted to mend me, and you'd be doing plenty if you helped me out," I said quietly, without his hearing.

But since there was no time to waste in telling jokes, I said to him, enlightened by the Holy Spirit: "'Uncle,' I've lost a key of this type,[34] and I'm afraid my master will flog me. By your life, see whether among those you're carrying on you there's one that fits, and I'll pay you for it."

The angelic tinker began trying out one after another in the big bunch he was carrying, and I began helping him with my feeble prayers. Unexpectedly, I caught sight of the "face of God," as the saying is—that is, the loaves of bread—inside the box. When it was open, I said: "I have no money to give you for the key, but take your payment out of this."

---

34. Reading with other texts: "a key for this strongbox."

Él tomó un bodigo de aquéllos, el que mejor le pareció, y dándome mi llave, se fue muy contento, dejándome más a mí. Mas no toqué en nada por el presente, porque no fuese la falta sentida, y aun porque me vi de tanto bien señor parecióme que la hambre no se me osaba allegar. Vino el mísero de mi amo, y quiso Dios no miró en la oblada que el ángel había llevado.

Y otro día, en saliendo de casa, abro mi paraíso panal, y tomo entre las manos y dientes un bodigo, y en dos credos le hice invisible, no se me olvidando el arca abierta; y comienzo a barrer la casa con mucha alegría, pareciéndome con aquel remedio remediar dende en adelante la triste vida. Y así estuve con ello aquel día y otro gozoso. Mas no estaba en mi dicha que me durase mucho aquel descanso, porque luego, al tercero día, me vino la terciana derecha.

Y fue que veo a deshora al que me mataba de hambre sobre nuestro arcaz, volviendo y revolviendo, contando y tornando a contar los panes. Yo disimulaba, y en mi secreta oración y devociones y plegarias, decía: "¡San Juan y ciégale!".

Después que estuvo un gran rato echando la cuenta, por días y dedos contando, dijo: —Si no tuviera a tan buen recado esta arca, yo dijera que me habían tomado della panes; pero de hoy más, sólo por cerrar la puerta a la sospecha, quiero tener buena cuenta con ellos: nueve quedan y un pedazo.

"¡Nuevas malas te dé Dios!", dije yo entre mí. Parecióme con lo que dijo pasarme el corazón con saeta de montero, y comenzóme el estómago a escarbar de hambre, viéndose puesto en la dieta pasada. Fue fuera de casa. Yo, por consolarme, abro el arca y, como vi el pan, comencélo de adorar, no osando recebillo. Contélos, si a dicha el lacerado se errara, y hallé su cuenta más verdadera que yo quisiera. Lo más que yo pude hacer fue dar en ellos mil besos, y, lo más delicado que yo pude, del partido partí un poco al pelo que le estaba, y con aquél pasé aquel día, no tan alegre como el pasado.

Mas como la hambre creciese, mayormente que tenía el estómago hecho a más pan aquellos dos o tres días ya dichos, moría mala muerte; tanto, que otra cosa no hacía en viéndome solo sino abrir y cerrar el arca y contemplar en aquella cara de Dios, que

He took one of those rich loaves, the one that looked best to him, and, giving me my key, departed in great satisfaction, leaving me alone. But for the moment I didn't touch a thing, so that the shortage wouldn't be noticed. Besides, since I found that I was the owner of so much property, I felt as if hunger didn't dare assail me. My wretched master returned, and God willed that he failed to notice the offering loaf that the angel had taken.

The next day, when he left the house, I opened my breadly paradise, took a loaf in my hand and between my teeth, and made it invisible in the time it takes to recite the Apostles' Creed twice. I didn't forget to close the box. Starting to sweep the house in great glee, I felt that by that means I had bettered my sad life from that time forward. And I remained happy over it that day and the next. But my luck didn't allow that relief to last long for me, because right away, on the third day, I got a real case of tertian fever.[35]

It was like this: at an ill, unexpected moment I saw the man who was killing me with hunger bent over our strongbox, turning the loaves over and over and counting them again and again. Pretending ignorance, I kept saying in my silent prayers, devotions, and orisons: "Saint John, blind him!"

After he had stood there toting up the account for quite a while, reckoning up the days and counting on his fingers, he said: "If I didn't keep such a close watch on this box, I'd say that loaves have been taken out of it. But from today on, merely to shut the door on suspicion, I intend to keep a strict accounting of them. There are nine left and a piece."

"May God send you bad tidings!"[36] I said to myself. At his words I felt as if my heart had been pierced with a huntsman's heavy arrow, and my stomach began gnawing with hunger, finding itself restored to its past diet. He left the house. To console myself, I opened the box and, at sight of the bread, I began to worship it, since I didn't dare to receive it.[37] I counted the loaves to see if that wretch might have been mistaken, but I found his count more accurate than I liked. The most I could do was to give them a thousand kisses; and, as carefully as I could, I removed a little from the cut piece along the line of the cut. With it I spent that day, which wasn't as merry as the one before.

But as my hunger increased, especially because my stomach had become used to more bread on those above-mentioned two or three days, I was dying a miserable death; so much so, that whenever I found myself alone, all I did was open and shut the box and contem-

---

35. Which was treated by fasting.    36. The Spanish has an untranslatable word play on *nueve* ("nine") and *nuevas* ("tidings").    37. The terminology is that of Communion.

ansí dicen los niños. Mas el mesmo Dios, que socorre a los afligidos, viéndome en tal estrecho, trujo a mi memoria un pequeño remedio: que, considerando entre mí, dije: "Este arquetón es viejo y grande y roto por algunas partes, aunque pequeños agujeros. Puédese pensar que ratones, entrando en él, hacen daño a este pan. Sacarlo entero no es cosa conveniente, porque verá la falta el que en tanta me hace vivir. Esto bien se sufre."

Y comienzo a desmigajar el pan sobre unos no muy costosos manteles que allí estaban, y tomo uno y dejo otro, de manera que en cada cual de tres o cuatro desmigajé su poco. Después, como quien toma gragea, lo comí, y algo me consolé. Mas él, como viniese a comer y abriese el arca, vio el mal pesar, y sin duda creyó ser ratones los que el daño habían hecho, porque estaba muy al propio contrahecho de como ellos lo suelen hacer. Miró todo el arcaz de un cabo a otro y viole ciertos agujeros, por do sospechaba habían entrado. Llamóme diciendo: —¡Lázaro! ¡Mira, mira qué persecución ha venido aquesta noche por nuestro pan!

Yo híceme muy maravillado, preguntándole qué sería.

—¡Qué ha de ser! —dijo él—. Ratones, que no dejan cosa a vida.

Pusímonos a comer, y quiso Dios que aun en esto me fue bien, que me cupo más pan que la laceria que me solía dar, porque rayó con un cuchillo todo lo que pensó ser ratonado, diciendo: —Cómete eso, que el ratón cosa limpia es.

Y así, aquel día, añadiendo la ración del trabajo de mis manos (o de mis uñas, por mejor decir), acabamos de comer, aunque yo nunca empezaba.

Y luego me vino otro sobresalto, que fue verle andar solícito quitando clavos de las paredes y buscando tablillas, con las cuales clavó y cerró todos los agujeros de la vieja arca.

"¡Oh Señor mío!", dije yo entonces. "¡A cuánta miseria y fortuna y desastres estamos puestos los nacidos y cuán poco turan los placeres de esta nuestra trabajosa vida! Heme aquí que pensaba con este pobre y triste remedio remediar y pasar mi laceria, y estaba ya cuanto que alegre y de buena ventura. Mas no quiso mi desdicha, despertando a este lacerado de mi amo y poniéndole más diligencia de la que él de suyo se tenía (pues los míseros por la mayor parte nunca de aquélla carecen), agora, cerrando los agujeros del arca, ciérrase la puerta a mi consuelo y la abriese a mis trabajos."

plate that "face of God," as children call it. But God Himself, who aids the afflicted, seeing me in such straits, recalled to my mind a small relief: I reflected on the situation and said: "This box is big, old, and broken in several spots, even though the holes are small. It might be thought that mice are getting in and damaging this bread. To take it out in one piece isn't appropriate, because the man who gives me such short measure will see the shortage. This way is tolerable."

And I began to crumble the bread onto some none-too-costly tablecloths that were on hand, taking one loaf and leaving another, in such a way that I crumbled away a little bit from each of three or four of them. Then, like someone enjoying fancy preserves,[38] I ate the crumbs and cheered up a little. But when he was ready for dinner and opened the box, he observed the misfortune, and certainly believed that mice had done the damage, because I had imitated in a very natural way their manner of doing so. He looked at the entire box from one end to the other, and saw certain holes through which he suspected they had got in. He called me over and said: "Lázaro! Look, see what an infliction our bread suffered last night!"

I pretended to be greatly surprised, asking him what it could be.

"What it can be!" he said. "Mice, which don't spare a thing."

We started to eat, and God willed that even that was to my benefit, because more bread fell to my lot than the pittance he ordinarily gave me, since with a knife he scraped away everything he thought was mouse-eaten, saying: "Eat this, for mice are clean animals."

And so, that day, adding in the portion due to the work of my hands (or my fingernails, to be more exact), we finished dining, although I generally never even began.

And right away I got another scare: I saw him go around busily removing nails from the walls and looking for little boards, which he nailed to the old box, closing up all the holes.

"Oh, Lord!" I then said. "How much misery, misfortune, and disaster we mortals are exposed to, and how brief a time the pleasures in this laborious life of ours last! Here I was, thinking that, by this poor, wretched means, I could relieve and bear my hunger, and I was a little cheerful and fortunate. But my bad luck wouldn't allow it: it woke up my stingy master and made him even more careful than he was by nature (for misers are generally never lacking in such solicitude), so that now, by closing the holes in the box, he is closing the door to my solace and opening it to my travails."

---

38. Or: "sugar-coated almonds."

Así lamentaba yo, en tanto que mi solícito carpintero, con muchos clavos y tablillas, dio fin a sus obras, diciendo: —Agora, donos traidores ratones, conviéneos mudar propósito, que en esta casa mala medra tenéis.

De que salió de su casa, voy a ver la obra, y hallé que no dejó en la triste y vieja arca agujero ni aun por donde le pudiese entrar un mosquito. Abro con mi desaprovechada llave, sin esperanza de sacar provecho, y vi los dos o tres panes comenzados, los que mi amo creyó ser ratonados, y dellos todavía saqué alguna laceria, tocándolos muy ligeramente, a uso de esgremidor diestro. Como la necesidad sea tan gran maestra, viéndome con tanta siempre noche y día estaba pensando la manera que ternía en sustentar el vivir. Y pienso, para hallar estos negros remedios, que me era luz la hambre, pues dicen que el ingenio con ella se avisa y al contrario con la hartura, y así era por cierto en mí.

Pues estando una noche desvelado en este pensamiento, pensando cómo me podría valer y aprovecharme del arcaz, sentí que mi amo dormía, porque lo mostraba con roncar y en unos resoplidos grandes que daba cuando estaba durmiendo. Levantéme muy quedito, y habiendo en el día pensado lo que había de hacer y dejado un cuchillo viejo que por allí andaba en parte do le hallase, voyme al triste arcaz, y, por do había mirado tener menos defensa, le acometí con el cuchillo, que a manera de barreno dél usé. Y como la antiquísima arca, por ser de tantos años, la hallase sin fuerza y corazón, antes muy blanda y carcomida, luego se me rindió, y consintió en su costado, por mi remedio, un buen agujero. Esto hecho, abro muy paso la llagada arca y, al tiento, del pan que hallé partido, hice según de yuso está escrito. Y con aquello algún tanto consolado, tornando a cerrar, me volví a mis pajas, en las cuales reposé y dormí un poco. Lo cual yo hacía mal y echábalo al no comer. Y ansí sería, porque, cierto, en aquel tiempo no me debían de quitar el sueño los cuidados de el rey de Francia.

Otro día fue por el señor mi amo visto el daño, así del pan como del agujero que yo había hecho, y comenzó a dar a los

That is how I lamented while my industrious carpenter, with all those nails and boards, completed his work and said: "Now, my lords, you villainous mice, you've got to change your plan, because you won't prosper in this house."

After he went out, I went over to examine the job he had done, and I found that he hadn't left in the miserable old box a hole big enough for even a gnat to get in. I opened it with my now superfluous key, with no hope of deriving any benefit, and looked at the two or three tampered-with loaves, the ones my master thought were mouse-eaten; I was still able to remove a tiny amount from them, handling them very gently, like a skillful fencer. Since necessity is such a great teacher, finding myself in the midst of it, I kept pondering day and night on the means to stay alive. And I believe that, if I discovered those puny solutions, it was because hunger enlightened me, for they say that it sharpens a man's wits, and a full belly does the opposite; and it was certainly so in my case.

Well, lying awake with these thoughts one night, thinking of ways to help myself and take advantage of the box, I noticed that my master was asleep, since he indicated it with his snoring and the heavy breaths he took while sleeping. I got up very quietly; having imagined during the day what I needed to do, and having left an old knife that was on hand in a place where I could find it, I went up to that miserable box and, in the spot where I had noticed it was least protected, I attacked it with the knife, which I used like a drill. And since I found the very old box, with all those years on its head, without strength or courage to resist, but rather very soft and worm-eaten, it surrendered to me at once and allowed me to bore a good-sized hole in its side, for my relief. Having done this, I opened the wounded box and, by touch, I subjected the loaves that I found already started to the manipulations I described earlier. Consoling myself with that to some extent, I locked the box again and returned to my straw pallet, where I rested and slept a little. I slept badly, blaming this on my hunger. And it must have been so, because at that age even the worries of the king of France[39] shouldn't have robbed me of my sleep.

The next day, the damage was seen by my lord and master, both the nibbled bread and the hole I had made; he started wishing that the

---

39. Probably just a general expression, but some commentators have thought this was a specific reference to the imprisonment of François I after losing the battle of Pavia in 1525. These commentators then drew corresponding conclusions as to the time when *Lazarillo de Tormes* was written, or when the action of the story takes place, or both.

diablos los ratones y decir: —¿Qué diremos a esto? ¡Nunca haber sentido ratones en esta casa sino agora! —Y sin duda debía de decir verdad, porque si casa había de haber en el reino justamente de ellos privilegiada, aquélla, de razón, había de ser, porque no suelen morar donde no hay qué comer. Torna a buscar clavos por la casa y por las paredes, y tablillas a atapárselos. Venida la noche y su reposo, luego era yo puesto en pie con mi aparejo, y cuantos él tapaba de día destapaba yo de noche.

En tal manera fue y tal priesa nos dimos, que sin duda por esto se debió decir: "Donde una puerta se cierra, otra se abre". Finalmente, parecíamos tener a destajo la tela de Penélope, pues cuanto él tejía de día rompía yo de noche, ca en pocos días y noches pusimos la pobre despensa de tal forma, que quien quisiera propiamente della hablar, más corazas viejas de otro tiempo que no arcaz la llamara, según la clavazón y tachuelas sobre sí tenía.

De que vio no le aprovechar nada su remedio, dijo: —Este arcaz está tan mal tratado, y es de madera tan vieja y flaca, que no habrá ratón a quien se defienda. Y va ya tal, que si andamos más con él nos dejará sin guarda. Y aun lo peor que, aunque hace poca, todavía hará falta faltando y me pondrá en costa de tres o cuatro reales. El mejor remedio que hallo, pues el de hasta aquí no aprovecha: armaré por de dentro a estos ratones malditos.

Luego buscó prestada una ratonera, y con cortezas de queso que a los vecinos pedía, contino el gato estaba armado dentro del arca. Lo cual era para mí singular auxilio, porque, puesto caso que yo no había menester muchas salsas para comer, todavía me holgaba con las cortezas del queso que de la ratonera sacaba, y, sin esto, no perdonaba el ratonar del bodigo.

Como hallase el pan ratonado y el queso comido y no cayese el ratón que lo comía, dábase al diablo, preguntaba a los vecinos qué podría ser comer el queso y sacarlo de la ratonera y no caer ni quedar dentro el ratón y hallar caída la trampilla del gato. Acordaron los vecinos no ser el ratón el que este daño hacía, porque no fuera menos de haber caído alguna vez. Díjole un vecino:

—En vuestra casa yo me acuerdo que solía andar una culebra, y ésta debe de ser sin duda. Y lleva razón, que, como es larga, tiene lugar de tomar el cebo, y aunque la coja la trampilla encima, como no entre toda dentro, tórnase a salir.

mice would go to the Devil, and said: "What can I say about this? I never noticed mice in this house until now!" And he must surely have been telling the truth, because if any house in the kingdom should have been rightly spared by them, that one should have been by rights because they usually don't live where there's nothing to eat. Again he looked for nails in the house and on the walls and boards to cover the hole. When night came and he fell asleep, I was immediately on my feet, seizing my opportunity, and as many holes as he covered by day I uncovered at night.

In this manner, it was surely because we acted with such urgency that the saying arose: "When one door closes, another opens." In short, we seemed to be doing piecework on Penelope's web, because all that he wove in the daytime I undid at night; in a few days and nights we had reduced the poor breadbox to such a state that anyone wishing to describe it accurately would have called it an old piece of armor from ancient days, rather than a strongbox, it was so full of nails and studs.

Once he had seen that his remedy wasn't helping him at all, he said: "This strongbox has been so manhandled, and its wood is so old and weak that it won't be able to withstand any mouse. It's already in such bad shape that, if we do any more to it, it will leave us without protection. Even worse is this: as little protection as it affords, even that will be gone if the box goes, and I'd have to spend three or four *reales* to replace it. The best solution I can think of, since none have worked so far, is to put a trap inside to catch these damned mice."

At once he sought the loan of a mousetrap and, with cheese rinds that he asked the neighbors for, the mechanical "cat" was constantly at the ready inside the box. This was remarkably advantageous to me, because, even though I didn't need fancy sauces to raise an appetite, nevertheless I was happy to have the cheese rinds that I took out of the mousetrap and, in addition, I didn't leave off "nibbling" at the bread.

On finding the bread "mouse-eaten," the cheese devoured, but no trace of the mouse who was eating it, he became furious and asked the neighbors how it could be that the cheese was eaten and removed from the mousetrap while the mouse wasn't caught and captured although the trap was sprung. The neighbors opined that it wasn't a mouse that was doing this damage, because it would surely have been caught one time or another. A neighbor told him:

"I recall that a snake used to roam around in your house, and the snake must surely be doing this. It stands to reason that, being long, it's able to snatch the bait and, even though the trap snaps shut on it, it can get out again because it's not completely inside."

Cuadró a todos lo que aquél dijo y alteró mucho a mi amo, y dende en adelante no dormía tan a sueño suelto, que cualquier gusano de la madera que de noche sonase pensaba ser la culebra que le roía el arca. Luego era puesto en pie, y con un garrote que a la cabecera, desde que aquello le dijeron, ponía, daba en la pecadora del arca grandes garrotazos, pensando espantar la culebra. A los vecinos despertaba con el estruendo que hacía y a mí no dejaba dormir. Íbase a mis pajas y trastornábalas, y a mí con ellas, pensando que se iba para mí y se envolvía en mis pajas o en mi sayo, porque le decían que de noche acaecía a estos animales, buscando calor, irse a las cunas donde están criaturas y aun mordellas y hacerles peligrar.

Yo las más veces hacía del dormido, y en la mañana decíame él: —¿Esta noche, mozo, no sentiste nada? Pues tras la culebra anduve, y aun pienso se ha de ir para ti a la cama, que son muy frías y buscan calor.

—Plega a Dios que no me muerda —decía yo—, que harto miedo le tengo.

Desta manera andaba tan elevado y levantado del sueño, que, mi fe, la culebra (o culebro, por mejor decir), no osaba roer de noche ni levantarse al arca; mas de día, mientras estaba en la iglesia o por el lugar, hacía mis saltos. Los cuales daños viendo él, y el poco remedio que les podía poner, andaba de noche, como digo, hecho trasgo.

Yo hube miedo que con aquellas diligencias no me topase con la llave, que debajo de las pajas tenía, y pareciome lo más seguro metella de noche en la boca. Porque ya, desde que viví con el ciego, la tenía tan hecha bolsa, que me acaeció tener en ella doce o quince maravedís, todo en medias blancas, sin que me estorbasen el comer, porque de otra manera no era señor de una blanca, que el maldito ciego no cayese con ella, no dejando costura ni remiendo que no me buscaba muy a menudo.

Pues ansí como digo, metía cada noche la llave en la boca y dormía sin recelo que el brujo de mi amo cayese con ella; mas cuando la desdicha ha de venir, por demás es diligencia. Quisieron mis hados (o, por mejor decir, mis pecados) que una noche que estaba durmiendo, la llave se me puso en la boca, que abierta debía tener, de tal manera y postura, que el aire y resoplo que yo durmiendo echaba salía por lo hueco de la llave, que de cañuto era, y silbaba, según mi desastre quiso, muy recio, de

Everyone agreed with that man's opinion, which greatly upset my master; from then on he no longer slept so soundly, but whenever he heard any termite making a sound at night, he thought it was the snake gnawing his box. He was up on his feet at once, and with a cudgel that he kept at the head of his bed ever since the neighbors had told him that, he would deal the wretched box heavy blows, thinking he was frightening the snake. He used to wake up the neighbors with the racket he made, and he didn't let me sleep, either. He would come up to my straw pallet and turn it over, and me with it, imagining that the snake was coming to me and concealing itself in my pallet or my shirt, because they told him that at night those animals, in search of warmth, sometimes entered cradles containing infants, whom they might even bite, causing them danger.

Most of the time I pretended to be asleep, and in the morning he'd say: "Boy, didn't you notice anything last night? I was searching for the snake, and I even think it must get in bed with you, because they suffer from the cold and look for warm places."

"I hope to God it doesn't bite me," I would say, "because I'm scared stiff of it."

And so, he went around so distraught and deprived of sleep that, by my faith, the snake (a male snake, to be exact) didn't dare gnaw at night or climb up to the box; but in the daytime, while he was in church or in town, I continued my pilfering. Seeing this damage and the uselessness of his countermeasures, he went around at night like a poltergeist, as I've said.

I was afraid that, with all the pains he was taking, he might find my key, which I kept in the straw of my pallet, and I thought it was safer to keep it in my mouth at night. Ever since my days with the blind man, I had converted my mouth into such an ample purse that at times I had twelve or fifteen *maravedís'* worth of half-*blancas* in it, without having any trouble eating, because otherwise I couldn't hold onto a *blanca* without that damned blind man finding it, since he frequently searched every seam and patch on me.

Well, as I said, every night I put the key in my mouth and slept without the fear of my sorcerer master finding it; but when misfortune is slated, prudence is futile. My destiny (or, to be more exact, my sins) willed that, one night as I lay asleep, the key assumed such a position in my mouth, which must have been open, that the air and breath I exhaled in my sleep emerged through the hollow of the key, which had a tubular stem, and it whistled very loud, as my unlucky star would have it, so that my startled master heard it and must surely have

tal manera, que el sobresaltado de mi amo lo oyó, y creyó sin duda ser el silbo de la culebra, y cierto lo debía parecer.

Levantóse muy paso con su garrote en la mano, y al tiento y sonido de la culebra se llegó a mí con mucha quietud por no ser sentido de la culebra. Y como cerca se vio, pensó que allí, en las pajas do yo estaba echado, al calor mío se había venido. Levantando bien el palo, pensando tenerla debajo y darle tal garrotazo que la matase, con toda su fuerza me descargó en la cabeza un tan gran golpe, que sin ningún sentido y muy mal descalabrado me dejó.

Como sintió que me había dado, según yo debía hacer gran sentimiento con el fiero golpe, contaba él que se había llegado a mí y, dándome grandes voces llamándome, procuró recordarme. Mas, como me tocase con las manos, tentó la mucha sangre que se me iba, y conoció el daño que me había hecho. Y con mucha priesa fue a buscar lumbre, y llegando con ella, hallóme quejando, todavía con mi llave en la boca, que nunca la desamparé, la mitad fuera, bien de aquella manera que debía estar al tiempo que silbaba con ella.

Espantado el matador de culebras qué podría ser aquella llave, miróla, sacándomela del todo de la boca, y vio lo que era, porque en las guardas nada de la suya diferenciaba. Fue luego a proballa, y con ella probó el maleficio. Debió de decir el cruel cazador: "El ratón y culebra que me daban guerra y me comían mi hacienda he hallado".

De lo que sucedió en aquellos tres días siguientes ninguna fe daré, porque los tuve en el vientre de la ballena, más de cómo esto que he contado oí, después que en mí torné, decir a mi amo, el cual, a cuantos allí venían lo contaba por extenso.

A cabo de tres días yo torné en mi sentido, y vime echado en mis pajas, la cabeza toda emplastada y llena de aceites y ungüentos, y espantado dije: —¿Qué es esto?

Respondióme el cruel sacerdote: —A fe que los ratones y culebras que me destruían ya los he cazado. —Y miré por mí, y vime tan maltratado, que luego sospeché mi mal.

A esta hora entró una vieja que ensalmaba, y los vecinos. Y comiénzanme a quitar trapos de la cabeza y curar el garrotazo.

taken it for the hissing of the snake; and, no doubt, it must have sounded like it.

He got up very quietly, his cudgel in his hand, and, groping his way in the direction of the snake's hiss, he came up to me, keeping very still so the snake wouldn't hear him. When he found he was close, he imagined it had sought the warmth of my body in the pallet where I was lying. Raising his cudgel high in the air, thinking the snake was at his feet and intending to give it a blow strong enough to kill it, with all his might he delivered such a hard blow to my head that he left me unconscious and with a battered head.

When he sensed that he had struck me, since I must have reacted violently to that fierce blow, he realized that I was the one he had hit, and, calling my name out loud, he tried to bring me to. But when he touched me, he felt all the blood that was pouring out of me and he became aware of how badly he had injured me. In great haste he went to get a light; returning with it, he found me moaning, with the key still in my mouth, because I had never lost hold of it. It was protruding halfway, just as it must have been when I whistled through it.

The snake hunter, worried over what that key could be, looked at it, removing it entirely from my mouth, and recognized it for what it was, since its wards were no different from those on his own. He went at once to try it out, and with it he ascertained the true nature of the evil spell he had been under. The cruel hunter must have said: "I have found the mouse and the snake that were waging war on me and eating my property."

Since I spent the next three days "in the belly of the whale," all I will recount about what happened during that time is what I heard my master say after I came to, because he narrated the whole thing in detail to every visitor.[40]

At the end of three days I was conscious again, and I found myself stretched out on my pallet, my head all plastered and full of oils and ointments. Frightened, I said: "What's this?"

The cruel priest replied: "I assure you I've driven away the mice and snakes that were eating me out of house and home." I looked at myself and saw myself in such a bad condition that I immediately guessed at my misfortune.

At that moment, a female quack doctor and the neighbors came in. They began to remove cloths from my head and tend to the cudgel

---

40. This involved sentence has also been interpreted differently, but the general sense is clear.

Y como me hallaron vuelto en mi sentido, holgáronse mucho, y dijeron: —Pues ha tornado en su acuerdo, placerá a Dios no será nada.

Ahí tornaron de nuevo a contar mis cuitas y a reirlas, y yo, pecador, a llorarlas. Con todo esto, diéronme de comer, que estaba transido de hambre, y apenas me pudieron remediar. Y ansí, de poco en poco, a los quince días me levanté y estuve sin peligro (mas no sin hambre) y medio sano.

Luego otro día que fui levantado, el señor mi amo me tomó por la mano y sacóme la puerta afuera, y puesto en la calle, díjome:

—Lázaro, de hoy más eres tuyo y no mío. Busca amo y vete con Dios. Que yo no quiero en mi compañía tan diligente servidor. No es posible sino que hayas sido mozo de ciego.

Y santiguándose de mí, como si yo estuviera endemoniado, tórnase a meter en casa y cierra su puerta.

## TRATADO TERCERO

### Cómo Lázaro se asentó con un escudero y de lo que le acaeció con él

Desta manera me fue forzado sacar fuerzas de flaqueza, y poco a poco, con ayuda de las buenas gentes, di comigo en esta insigne ciudad de Toledo, adonde, con la merced de Dios, dende a quince días se me cerró la herida. Y mientras estaba malo, siempre me daban alguna limosna; mas después que estuve sano, todos me decían: —Tú, bellaco y gallofero eres. Busca, busca un amo a quien sirvas.

—¿Y dónde se hallará ése —decía yo entre mí—, si Dios agora de nuevo, como crió el mundo, no le criase?

Andando así discurriendo de puerta en puerta, con harto poco remedio (porque ya la caridad se subió al cielo), topóme Dios con un escudero que iba por la calle, con razonable vestido, bien peinado, su paso y compás en orden. Miróme y yo a él, y díjome: —Mochacho, ¿buscas amo?

Yo le dije: —Sí, señor.

wound. Since they found me in my senses again, they were very pleased and said: "Since he's awake again, God willing, it won't be serious."

Then they began telling of my troubles again and laughing at them, while I, the sinner, bewailed them. Nevertheless, they gave me some food—I was absolutely starved—but they were scarcely able to serve my turn.[41] And so, little by little, in two weeks I became strong enough to get up and be out of danger (but not free from hunger) and half-cured.

The very day after I got out of bed, my lord and master took me by the hand and led me out the door. Once I was in the street, he said:

"Lázaro, from today on, you belong to yourself and not to me. Look for a master and go with God. Because I don't want such a diligent servant to keep me company. There isn't the slightest doubt that you've been a blind man's helper."

He crossed himself at the sight of me, as if I were devil-ridden, went back into his house, and locked his door.

## CHAPTER THREE

### How Lázaro Was Employed by a Nobleman, and What Happened to Him in His Company

And so I was strongly compelled to derive strength from weakness; little by little, with the aid of kind people, I arrived in this famous city of Toledo, where, with the grace of God, my wound healed completely in two further weeks. While I was still sick, I always received a little alms, but after I was well, everyone said to me: "You're a cadger and a panhandler. Look for a master to serve."

"And where am I to find one," I said to myself, "unless God creates one now out of whole cloth, the way He created the world?"

As I was scurrying this way from door to door, receiving mighty little aid (because charity has now retreated to the skies), God made me meet a squire who was walking in the street, reasonably well dressed, well groomed, and with an elegant pace and bearing. He looked at me, and I at him, and he said: "Boy, are you searching for a master?"

I replied: "Yes, sir."

---

41. Another 1554 edition has *demediar* ("to give me even half of what I needed").

—Pues vente tras mí —me respondió—, que Dios te ha hecho merced en topar comigo; alguna buena oración rezaste hoy.

Y seguíle, dando gracias a Dios por lo que le oí, y también que me parecía, según su hábito y continente, ser el que yo había menester.

Era de mañana cuando este mi tercero amo topé; y llevóme tras sí gran parte de la ciudad. Pasábamos por las plazas do se vendía pan y otras provisiones. Yo pensaba (y aun deseaba) que allí me quería cargar de lo que se vendía, porque ésta era propria hora, cuando se suele proveer de lo necesario; más muy a tendido paso pasaba por estas cosas. "Por ventura no lo vee aquí a su contento —decía yo—, y querrá que lo compremos en otro cabo".

Desta manera anduvimos hasta que dio las once. Entonces se entró en la iglesia mayor, y yo tras él, y muy devotamente le vi oír misa y los otros oficios divinos, hasta que todo fue acabado y la gente ida. Entonces salimos de la iglesia; a buen paso tendido comenzamos a ir por una calle abajo. Yo iba el más alegre del mundo en ver que no nos habíamos ocupado en buscar de comer. Bien consideré que debía ser hombre, mi nuevo amo, que se proveía en junto, y que ya la comida estaría a punto y tal como yo la deseaba y aun la había menester.

En este tiempo dio el reloj la una después de medio día, y llegamos a una casa ante la cual mi amo se paró, y yo con él, y derribando el cabo de la capa sobre el lado izquierdo, sacó una llave de la manga, y abrió su puerta, y entramos en casa. La cual tenía la entrada obscura y lóbrega de tal manera, que parece que ponía temor a los que en ella entraban, aunque dentro della estaba un patio pequeño y razonables cámaras.

Desque fuimos entrados, quita de sobre sí su capa, y preguntando si tenía las manos limpias, la sacudimos y doblamos, y muy limpiamente, soplando un poyo que allí estaba, la puso en él; y hecho esto, sentóse cabo della, preguntándome muy por extenso de dónde era, y cómo había venido a aquella ciudad. Y yo le di más larga cuenta que quisiera, porque me parecía más conveniente hora de mandar poner la mesa y escudillar la olla, que de lo que me pedía. Con todo eso, yo le satisfice de mi persona lo mejor que mentir supe, diciendo mis bienes y callando lo demás, porque me parecía no ser para en cámara. Esto hecho, estuvo ansí un poco, y yo luego vi mala señal, por ser ya casi las dos y no le ver más aliento de comer que a un muerto. Después desto,

"Then follow me," he answered, "for God has shown you grace by making you meet me; you must have recited some good prayer today."

I followed him, thanking God for what I heard him say, and also because, seeing his attire and bearing, I thought he was the master I needed.

It was in the morning when I met this third master of mine; he led me after him through a large part of the city. We passed through the squares where bread and other provisions were sold. I kept thinking (and wishing) that he would load me down there with the food that was for sale, because it was the right time, when people usually lay in supplies; but he passed by such spots with huge strides. "Maybe he doesn't see what he likes here," I said to myself, "and he wants us to buy it elsewhere."

We continued that way until the clock struck eleven. Then he entered the cathedral and I followed. I saw him hear Mass and the other religious services very piously, until it was all over and the people were gone. Then we left the church; we started to descend a street at a good clip. As I walked, I was the happiest person in the world, when I saw that we had spent no time looking for food. I imagined that my new master must be a man who purchased foodstuffs in quantity, and that our dinner would be ready for us, and of the sort I wished and, in fact, needed.

At that moment the clock struck 1 P.M., and we arrived at a house in front of which my master stopped, as I did, too. Throwing back one corner of his cloak over his left shoulder, he drew a key out of his sleeve and opened his door, and we went in. The entrance to the house was so dark and gloomy that I thought it must frighten anyone coming in, even though inside it there was a small patio and decent rooms.

Once we were inside, he took off his cloak; after he asked me if my hands were clean, we shook it out and folded it, and, blowing the dust off a stone bench there, he placed it on it very neatly. After that, he sat down beside it and asked me in great detail where I was from and how I had come to that city. I gave him a longer account than I liked, because I thought it was a more suitable hour for ordering the table to be set and the stew to be dished out than to do what he demanded of me. Anyway, I satisfied him as to my personal qualities, lying as much as I could, declaring my good points and keeping quiet about the rest, because I thought it might be impolite or inopportune. After that, he remained there for a while, which I immediately took as a bad sign, because it was now nearly two and I didn't see him anymore

consideraba aquel tener cerrada la puerta con llave, ni sentir
arriba ni abajo pasos de viva persona por la casa; todo lo que yo
había visto eran paredes, sin ver en ella silleta, ni tajo, ni banco,
ni mesa, ni aun tal arcaz como el de marras. Finalmente, ella
parecía casa encantada. Estando así, díjome: —Tú, mozo, ¿has
comido?

—No, señor —dije yo—, que aunque no eran dadas las ocho
cuando con Vuestra Merced encontré.

—Pues, aunque de mañana, yo había almorzado, y cuando
ansí como algo, hágote saber que hasta la noche me estoy ansí.
Por eso, pásate como pudieres, que después cenaremos.

Vuestra Merced crea, cuando esto le oí, que estuve en poco
de caer de mi estado, no tanto de hambre como por conocer de
todo en todo la fortuna serme adversa. Allí se me representaron
de nuevo mis fatigas, y torné a llorar mis trabajos; allí se me vino
a la memoria la consideración que hacía cuando me pensaba ir
del clérigo, diciendo que, aunque aquel era desventurado y
mísero, por ventura toparía con otro peor; finalmente, allí lloré
mi trabajosa vida pasada y mi cercana muerte venidera. Y con
todo, disimulando lo mejor que pude:

—Señor, mozo soy que no me fatigo mucho por comer, bendito Dios: deso me podré yo alabar entre todos mis iguales por
de mejor garganta, y ansí fui yo loado della fasta hoy día de los
amos que yo he tenido.

—Virtud es ésa —dijo él—, y por eso te querré yo más:
porque el hartar es de los puercos, y el comer regladamente es
de los hombres de bien.

"¡Bien te he entendido!", dije yo entre mí. "¡Maldita tanta
medicina y bondad como aquestos mis amos que yo hallo hallan
en la hambre!".

Púseme a un cabo del portal, y saqué unos pedazos de pan del
seno, que me habían quedado de los de por Dios. Él, que vio
esto, díjome: —Ven acá, mozo. ¿Qué comes?

Yo lleguéme a él y mostréle el pan. Tomóme él un pedazo, de
tres que eran, el mejor y más grande, y díjome: —Por mi vida
que parece éste buen pan.

—¡Y cómo agora —dije yo—, señor, es bueno!

—Sí, a fe —dijo él—. ¿Adónde lo hubiste? ¿Si es amasado de
manos limpias?

—No sé yo eso —le dije—; mas a mí no me pone asco el sabor
dello.

eager to eat than a dead man. Next, I reflected on the fact that he kept the door locked, and that I couldn't hear the steps of a living soul in the house upstairs or downstairs. All I had seen was bare walls; the house didn't contain a chair, a stool, a bench, a table, or even a strong-box like my last master's. In short, it seemed to be under a spell. While we were that way, he said: "Boy, have you dined?"

"No, sir," I said, "because it wasn't even eight when I met Your Honor."

"Well, even though it was early in the morning, I had already break-fasted, and when I eat something that way, let me tell you that it holds me until nighttime. And so, get along as best you can, because we'll have supper later on."

Your Honor may well believe that, when I heard him say this, I came close to fainting away, not so much from hunger as from the re-alization that Fortune was thoroughly hostile to me. Then I recalled all my troubles, and I began to lament my suffering again; then I re-membered the reflection I had made when I considered abandoning the priest: even though he was disastrous and wretched, I might come across someone worse. In short, at that moment I bewailed my sor-rowful past life and my imminent death. Nevertheless, hiding my feel-ings as much as I could, I said:

"Sir, I'm a boy who doesn't worry much about eating, thank God; among all my peers I can boast of being the least gluttonous, and I've been praised for that to this very day by my different masters."

"That's a virtue," he said, "and I'll like you all the better for it: be-cause it's only pigs that stuff themselves, while decent people eat mod-erately."

"I hear you coming!" I said to myself. "Damn the healthfulness and the virtue that the masters whom I find find in hunger!"

I went and stood at one end of the entrance hall and took out of my shirt front a few pieces of bread left over from the alms I had re-ceived. Seeing this, he said: "Come here, boy. What are you eating?"

I walked up to him and showed him the bread. He took a piece from me, the best and biggest of the three I had, and said: "Upon my life, this looks like good bread."

"And how good it is now!" I said.

"Yes, by my faith," said he. "Where did you get it? Was it kneaded by clean hands?"

"I don't know about that," I said, "but the taste of it doesn't disgust *me*."

—Así plega a Dios —dijo el pobre de mi amo. Y llevándolo a
la boca, comenzó a dar en él tan fieros bocados como yo en lo
otro. —Sabrosísimo pan está —dijo—, por Dios.

Y como le sentí de qué pie cosqueaba, dime priesa, porque le
vi en disposición, si acababa antes que yo, se comediría a ayu-
darme a lo que me quedase. Y con esto acabamos casi a una. Y
mi amo comenzó a sacudir con las manos unas pocas de migajas,
y bien menudas, que en los pechos se le habían quedado. Y
entró en una camareta que allí estaba, y sacó un jarro desbocado
y no muy nuevo, y desque hubo bebido, convidóme con él. Yo,
por hacer del continente, dije: —Señor, no bebo vino.

—Agua es —me respondió—; bien puedes beber.

Entonces tomé el jarro y bebí. No mucho, porque de sed no
era mi congoja.

Ansí estuvimos hasta la noche, hablando en cosas que me preguntaba, a las cuales yo le respondí lo mejor que supe. En este
tiempo metióme en la cámara donde estaba el jarro de que bebimos y díjome: —Mozo, párate allí, y verás cómo hacemos esta
cama, para que la sepas hacer de aquí adelante.

Púseme de un cabo y él del otro, y hecimos la negra cama, en
la cual no había mucho que hacer, porque ella tenía sobre unos
bancos un cañizo, sobre el cual estaba tendida la ropa, que por
no estar muy continuada a lavarse, no parecía colchón, aunque
servía dél, con harta menos lana que era menester. Aquél tendi-
mos, haciendo cuenta de ablandalle; lo cual era imposible,
porque de lo duro mal se puede hacer blando. El diablo del en-
jalma maldita la cosa tenía dentro de sí, que, puesto sobre el
cañizo, todas las cañas se señalaban, y parecían a lo proprio en-
trecuesto de flaquísimo puerco. Y sobre aquel hambriento
colchón, un alfamar del mesmo jaez, del cual el color yo no pude
alcanzar.

Hecha la cama y la noche venida, díjome: —Lázaro, ya es
tarde, y de aquí a la plaza hay gran trecho; también en esta ciudad andan muchos ladrones, que, siendo de noche, capean.
Pasemos como podamos y mañana, venido el día, Dios hará
merced; porque yo, por estar solo, no estoy proveído, antes, he
comido estos días por allá fuera; mas agora hacerlo hemos de
otra manera.

—Señor, de mí —dije yo— ninguna pena tenga Vuestra

"So may it please God," said my poor master. And, raising it to his mouth, he started to take the same wild bites out of it as I was doing out of the other piece. "By God, it's very tasty bread," he said.

Now that I realized where his weakness lay,[42] I began to rush, because I saw that, if he finished before I did, his mood was such that he would venture to help me with whatever I had left. And so we finished at nearly the same time. My master began to brush off a few tiny crumbs that had fallen onto his chest. Then he went into a little room there and brought out a jug with a chipped rim and not very new; after taking a drink from it, he offered me one. Pretending to be a teetotaler, I said: "Sir, I don't drink wine."

"It's water," he replied, "you can go ahead and drink it."

Then I took the jug and drank. Not much, because it wasn't thirst that was bothering me.

And so we remained until nightfall, discussing things he asked me about, while I gave the best answers I could. Then he led me into the room where the jug was that we drank out of, and he said: "Boy, stop here and watch how we make this bed, so you can do it from now on."

I stood at one end and he at the other, and we made that wretched bed, in which there wasn't much to make, because it consisted of a lattice of reeds placed on some benches. Over the reeds was placed the mattress, which, because it wasn't washed very regularly, didn't look like one though it was used as one; it was stuffed with far less wool than it required. We spread it out, imagining that we were softening it; but that was impossible, because hardness can't very well be transformed into softness. That devil of a mattress had hardly anything inside it, so that, when it was placed over the reed lattice, every individual reed stood out, the whole thing resembling an emaciated pig's backbone. And over that famished mattress, a blanket of the same kind, the color of which I couldn't make out.

When the bed was made and night had come, he said: "Lázaro, it's late now, and it's a long way from here to the market; besides, there are many robbers in this city who steal people's cloaks at night. Let's get through the night as best we can, and tomorrow, when it's light, God will be gracious to us; because, since I live alone, I have no food in the house; in fact, the last few days I've eaten out; but now we have to make different arrangements."

"Sir," I said, "Your Honor need have no worries about *me*, because

---

42. Literally: "which foot he limped on" (*cosquear* = modern *cojear*).

Merced, que bien sé pasar una noche y aun más, si es menester, sin comer.

—Vivirás más y más sano —me respondió—, porque, como decíamos hoy, no hay tal cosa en el mundo para vivir mucho, que comer poco.

"Si por esa vía es", dije entre mí, "nunca yo moriré, que siempre he guardado esa regla por fuerza, y aun espero, en mi desdicha, tenella toda mi vida".

Y acostóse en la cama, poniendo por cabecera las calzas y el jubón. Y mandóme echar a sus pies, lo cual yo hice. Mas maldito el sueño que yo dormí, porque las cañas y mis salidos huesos en toda la noche dejaron de rifar y encenderse, que con mis trabajos, males y hambre pienso que en mi cuerpo no había libra de carne, y también, como aquel día no había comido casi nada, rabiaba de hambre, la cual con el sueño no tenía amistad. Maldíjeme mil veces (Dios me lo perdone), y a mi ruin fortuna, allí lo más de la noche, y lo peor, no osándome revolver por no despertalle, pedí a Dios muchas veces la muerte.

La mañana venida levantámonos, y comienza a limpiar y sacudir sus calzas, y jubón, y sayo y capa. Y yo que le servía de pelillo. Y vístese muy a su placer, de espacio. Echéle aguamanos, peinóse, y puso su espada en el talabarte, y al tiempo que la ponía díjome:

—¡Oh, si supieses, mozo, qué pieza es ésta! No hay marco de oro en el mundo por que yo la diese; mas ansí, ninguna de cuantas Antonio hizo, no acertó a ponelle los aceros tan prestos como ésta los tiene.

Y sacóla de la vaina y tentóla con los dedos, diciendo: —Vesla aquí. Yo me obligo con ella a cercenar un copo de lana.

Y yo dije entre mí: "Y yo con mis dientes, aunque no son de acero, un pan de cuatro libras".

Tornóla a meter y ciñósela, y un sartal de cuentas gruesas del talabarte. Y con un paso sosegado y el cuerpo derecho, haciendo con él y con la cabeza muy gentiles meneos, echando el cabo de la capa sobre el hombro y a veces so el brazo, y poniendo la mano derecha en el costado, salió por la puerta, diciendo:

—Lázaro, mira por la casa en tanto que voy a oír misa, y haz la cama, y ve por la vasija de agua al río, que aquí bajo está; y

I'm well able to get through one night, and even more if necessary, without eating."

"You'll live longer and feel better," he replied, "because, as we were saying today, there's nothing in the world that prolongs life like eating frugally."

"If that's the way to do it," I said to myself, "I'll never die, because I've always been compelled to observe that rule, and I'm so unlucky that I expect to observe it as long as I live."

He lay down on the bed, using his breeches and doublet as a pillow. He ordered me to stretch out at his feet, which I did. But I'll be damned if I could sleep, because all night long the reeds and my protruding bones didn't stop fighting and arguing, since with my sorrows, misfortunes, and hunger I don't think there was a pound of flesh on my body. Besides, since I had eaten almost nothing all that day, I felt a ravenous hunger, which is no friend to sleep. I cursed myself a thousand times (may God forgive me for it) and I cursed my evil fortune, most of the night; the worst thing was that I didn't dare turn over so as not to wake him, and I asked God over and over to end my life.

When morning came, we got up and he started to clean and shake out his breeches, doublet, tunic, and cloak. I could only help him in trifling ways. He got dressed very much at his ease, slowly. I poured water over his hands, he combed, and attached his sword to his sword belt; while doing that, he said:

"Boy, if you only knew what a blade this is! I wouldn't exchange it for any half-pound of gold in the world, because, you see, in none of the ones that Antonio[43] made was he able to make the steel as responsive as in this one."

He drew it from its scabbard and touched its edge, saying: "Look here. I wager I could slice a tuft of wool with it."

I said to myself: "And even though my teeth aren't made of steel, I could cut through a four-pound loaf with them."

He returned the sword to its scabbard and girded it on, also hanging a rosary of thick beads from the sword belt. Then, at a calm pace, holding his body erect and moving it and his head very genteelly, throwing the end of his cloak over his shoulder and at times over his arm, and placing his right hand on his side, he went out the door, saying:

"Lázaro, look after the house while I go hear Mass, and make the bed, and go fill the water jug at the river, which is just below here; and

---

43. A famous swordsmith from the reign of Ferdinand and Isabella.

cierra la puerta con llave, no nos hurten algo, y ponla aquí al quicio, porque, si yo viniere en tanto, pueda entrar.

Y súbese por la calle arriba con tal gentil semblante y continente, que quien no le conociera pensara ser muy cercano pariente al conde de Arcos, o, a lo menos, camarero que le daba de vestir.

"¡Bendito seáis Vos, Señor", quedé yo diciendo, "que dais la enfermedad, y ponéis el remedio! ¿Quién encontrará a aquel mi señor que no piense, según el contento de sí lleva, haber anoche bien cenado y dormido en buena cama, y aun agora es de mañana, no le cuenten por muy bien almorzado? ¡Grandes secretos son, Señor, los que Vos hacéis y las gentes ignoran! ¿A quién no engañará aquella buena disposición y razonable capa y sayo? ¿Y quién pensara que aquel gentil hombre se pasó ayer todo el día sin comer con aquel mendrugo de pan, que su criado Lázaro trujo un día y una noche en el arca de su seno, do no se le podía pegar mucha limpieza, y hoy, lavándose las manos y cara, a falta de paño de manos se hacía servir de la halda del sayo? Nadie por cierto lo sospechara. ¡Oh, Señor, y cuántos de aquéstos debéis Vos tener por el mundo derramados, que padecen por la negra que llaman honra, lo que por Vos no sufrirán!".

Ansí estaba yo a la puerta, mirando y considerando estas cosas, y otras muchas, hasta que el señor mi amo traspuso la larga y angosta calle; y como lo vi trasponer, tornéme a entrar en casa, y en un credo la anduve toda, alto y bajo, sin hacer represa, ni hallar en qué. Hago la negra dura cama, y tomo el jarro, y doy comigo en el río, donde en una huerta vi a mi amo en gran recuesta con dos rebozadas mujeres, al parecer de las que en aquel lugar no hacen falta, antes muchas tienen por estilo de irse a las mañanicas del verano a refrescar y almorzar, sin llevar qué, por aquellas frescas riberas, con confianza que no ha de faltar quien se lo dé, según las tienen puestas en esta costumbre aquellos hidalgos del lugar.

Y como digo, él estaba entre ellas hecho un Macías, diciéndoles más dulzuras que Ovidio escribió. Pero, como sintieron

lock the door so nothing gets stolen, and put the key here in the door jamb, so that I can get in if I should arrive while you're out."

And up the street he went, with such a noble appearance and bearing that anyone who didn't know him would have thought he was a near relation of the Count of Arcos,[44] or at least the manservant who helped him dress.

"Blessings on You, Lord," I said as I remained behind, "for You send the illness and supply the cure. Who wouldn't think, meeting my master and seeing him so self-satisfied, that he had had a good supper last night and slept in a good bed, and that he had had a wonderful breakfast, early in the morning as it is? Lord, there are great mysteries that You perform and that people are unaware of! Who wouldn't be fooled by his good mood and his respectable cloak and tunic? And who would think that that gentleman spent all of yesterday eating nothing but that hard crust which his servant Lázaro had been carrying for a day and a night in the strongbox of his shirt front, where it couldn't have gotten too clean, or that today, when he washed his hands and face, he dried himself with the skirt of his tunic for want of a towel? Surely no one would suspect it. Oh, Lord, how many people like that you must have scattered around the world, who suffer on behalf of that misery they call honor things that they wouldn't suffer on Your behalf!"

I stood at the door that way, reflecting and pondering over these matters and many more, until my lord and master crossed the long, narrow street; and when I saw him disappear from sight, I went back into the house. In the time it takes to recite the Creed, I combed it all, upstairs and down, without stopping[45] or finding anything. I made the damned hard bed, and I took the jug and went to the river with it. In an orchard there I saw my master ardently wooing two women whose faces were concealed by their mantillas, and who seemed to be of the sort found in great numbers at that spot. In fact, many of them consider it fashionable on early mornings in summer to visit that cool riverbank to take the air and have breakfast, bringing along no money, because they're sure of finding someone to pay for it, since the local noblemen have accustomed them to it.

As I said, he was standing among them like a great lover,[46] telling them more sweet nothings than Ovid composed. When they realized

---

44. Another 1554 edition reads *Alarcos*, and some editors, believing that the "manservant" refers to a specific ballad (*romance*), read *Claros*.  45. Or: "seizing prey"; or: "finding a source for increasing my supplies."  46. Literally: "like Macías," a 14th-century Galician troubadour said to have died of love.

dél que estaba bien enternecido, no se les hizo de vergüenza
pedirle de almorzar con el acostumbrado pago.

Él, sintiéndose tan frío de bolsa cuanto estaba caliente del estómago, tomóle tal calofrío, que le robó la color del gesto, y
comenzó a turbarse en la plática, y a poner excusas no validas.
Ellas, que debían ser bien instituidas, como le sintieron la enfermedad, dejáronle para el que era.

Yo, que estaba comiendo ciertos tronchos de berzas, con los
cuales me desayuné, con mucha diligencia, como mozo nuevo,
sin ser visto de mi amo, torné a casa, de la cual pensé barrer alguna parte, que era bien menester; mas no hallé con qué.
Púseme a pensar qué haría, y parecióme esperar a mi amo hasta
que el día demediase, y si viniese y por ventura trajese algo que
comiésemos; mas en vano fue mi experiencia.

Desque vi ser las dos y no venía y la hambre me aquejaba,
cierro mi puerta y pongo la llave do mandó y tórnome a mi menester. Con baja y enferma voz y inclinadas mis manos en los
senos, puesto Dios ante mis ojos y la lengua en su nombre,
comienzo a pedir pan por las puertas y casas más grandes que
me parecía. Mas como yo este oficio le hobiese mamado en la
leche (quiero decir que con el gran maestro el ciego lo aprendí),
tan suficiente discípulo salí, que aunque en este pueblo no había
caridad ni el año fuese muy abundante, tan buena maña me di,
que antes que el reloj diese las cuatro ya yo tenía otras tantas libras de pan ensiladas en el cuerpo, y más de otras dos en las
mangas y senos. Volvíme a la posada, y al pasar por la Tripería
pedí a una de aquellas mujeres, y dióme un pedazo de uña de
vaca con otras pocas de tripas cocidas.

Cuando llegué a casa, ya el bueno de mi amo estaba en ella,
doblada su capa y puesta en el poyo, y él paseándose por el
patio. Como entro, vínose para mí. Pensé que me quería reñir
la tardanza, mas mejor lo hizo Dios. Preguntóme dó venía. Yo
le dije:

—Señor, hasta que dio las dos estuve aquí, y de que vi que
Vuestra Merced no venía, fuime por esa ciudad a encomen-
darme a las buenas gentes, y hanme dado esto que veis.

Mostréle el pan y las tripas, que en un cabo de la halda traía,
a la cual él mostró buen semblante, y dijo: —Pues esperado te

he was really amorous, they felt no shame in asking him to give them breakfast in return for the usual compensation.

He, realizing that his purse was as cold as his belly was hot, was seized with such a shiver that his face turned pale and he began to get tongue-tied and make feeble excuses. The women must have been very experienced, and when they realized what ailed him, they left him, knowing him for what he was.[47]

I had been making my breakfast on a few cabbage stalks; now, very diligently as befitting a new servant, I went back home without my master seeing me. I intended to sweep a part of the house, which really needed it, but I couldn't find anything to do it with. I started to think about what I should do, and I decided to await my master until midday, thinking he might come and perhaps bring something for us to eat. But my experiment was in vain.

When I saw that it was two o'clock and he wasn't coming, and I was feeling hunger pangs, I locked the door, put the key where he had told me, and returned to my first profession. With a weak, sick voice and my hands resting on my breast, with God before my eyes and His name on my tongue, I started to beg for bread at doorways and the houses I thought were richest. Since I had learned that business at my mother's knee (I mean, I was taught it by that great master, the blind man), I proved to be such an apt pupil that, even though the local people weren't charitable and it hadn't been a year of plenty, I exerted myself so successfully that before the clock struck four I had stored away that number of pounds of bread in my stomach, and over two pounds more in my sleeves and shirt front. I returned home and, while walking through the Tripería,[48] I begged from one of the women there, who gave me a piece of cow's foot with a little more boiled offal.

When I got home, my good master was already there, his cloak folded and placed on the stone bench; he was strolling in the patio. When I came in, he walked up to me. I thought he was going to bawl me out for being late, but God helped me. My master asked me where I was coming from. I said:

"Sir, I remained here until two o'clock and when I saw that Your Honor wasn't coming, I walked through the city, throwing myself on the mercy of the kind people, and you see what they gave me."

I showed him the bread and the offal, which I was carrying wrapped in one end of my shirt. He looked happy to see it, and said:

---

47. Or: "left him to the proper sort of doctor."    48. "Offal Street," today the Calle Sixto Ramón Parro, a little east of the Cathedral.

he a comer, y de que vi que no veniste, comí. Mas tú haces como hombre de bien en eso, que más vale pedillo por Dios que no hurtallo. Y ansí Él me ayude como ello me parece bien, y solamente te encomiendo no sepan que vives comigo, por lo que toca a mi honra; aunque bien creo que será secreto, según lo poco que en este pueblo soy conocido. ¡Nunca a él yo hubiera de venir!

—De eso pierda, señor, cuidado —le dije yo—, que maldito aquel que ninguno tiene de pedirme esa cuenta, ni yo de dalla.

—Agora, pues, come, pecador, que si a Dios place, presto nos veremos sin necesidad. Aunque te digo que después que en esta casa entré, nunca bien me ha ido; debe ser de mal suelo, que hay casas desdichadas y de mal pie, que a los que viven en ellas pegan la desdicha. Esta debe de ser, sin duda, dellas; mas yo te prometo, acabado el mes no quede en ella, aunque me la den por mía.

Sentéme al cabo del poyo, y porque no me tuviese por glotón, callé la merienda, y comienzo a cenar y morder en mis tripas y pan, y, disimuladamente, miraba al desventurado señor mío, que no partía sus ojos de mis faldas, que aquella sazón servían de plato. Tanta lástima haya Dios de mí como yo había dél, porque sentí lo que sentía, y muchas veces había por ello pasado, y pasaba cada día. Pensaba si sería bien comedirme a convidalle; mas, por me haber dicho que había comido, temíame no aceptaría el convite. Finalmente, yo deseaba aquel pecador ayudase a su trabajo del mío, y se desayunase como el día antes hizo, pues había mejor aparejo, por ser mejor la vianda y menos mi hambre.

Quiso Dios cumplir mi deseo, y aun pienso que el suyo, porque, como comencé a comer y él se andaba paseando, llegóse a mí y díjome:

—Dígote, Lázaro, que tienes en comer la mejor gracia que en mi vida vi a hombre, y que nadie te lo verá hacer que no le pongas gana aunque no la tenga.

"La muy buena que tú tienes", dije yo entre mí, "te hace parecer la mía hermosa".

Con todo, pareciome ayudarle pues se ayudaba y me abría camino para ello, y díjele: —Señor, el buen aparejo hace buen artífice; este pan está sabrosísimo, y esta uña de vaca tan bien cocida y sazonada, que no habrá a quién no convide con su sabor.

—¿Uña de vaca es?

"Well, I waited to eat until you were back, but once I saw you weren't coming, I had dinner. But in doing what you did, you've acted very respectably, because begging is better than stealing. May God help me, I think you've done the right thing. I only urge you not to let people know you're living with me, on account of my honor; though I'm sure it won't become common knowledge, because so few people here know me. I wish I never had come here!"

"Sir," I said, "put your mind to rest about that, because no one has any cause to question me about it, nor have I any to reply."

"Well, eat now, my poor boy, because, if God wills, we'll soon be out of hardship. Though I tell you that ever since I set foot in this house, things have never gone right for me; it must be built on evil soil, for there are unlucky and ill-omened houses that cause bad luck for whoever lives in them. This must surely be one. But I promise you that, when this month is up, I won't stay here even if they make me a gift of it."

I sat down on one end of the bench. So that he wouldn't consider me gluttonous, I said nothing about my midday meal, but started to have supper, biting into my offal and bread. I took sly looks at my unfortunate master, who couldn't tear his eyes away from the bottom of my shirt, which I was using as a plate at the moment. May God have as much pity on me as I had on him, because I felt what he was feeling, and had experienced it many a time, and experienced it daily. I wondered if it would be right to venture to invite him; but, since he had told me he had eaten, I was afraid he wouldn't accept the invitation. In short, I wished that that sinner would make use of my labors for his own necessities and would break his fast as he had done on the previous day, seeing that he had a better opportunity, the food being better and I less hungry.

God so willed it that my wish was granted, and I think his, too, because, when I started eating while he was walking up and down, he came up to me and said:

"I tell you, Lázaro, you eat as gracefully as I've ever seen anyone eat, and no one could watch you without getting an appetite even if he didn't have one."

"The fine one that you have," I said to myself, "makes you find mine attractive."

And so, I decided to help him since he was making an effort and showing me the way to do so, and I said: "Sir, a good opportunity makes a good craftsman; this bread is extremely tasty and this cow's foot is so well cooked and seasoned that no one could resist its flavor."

"It's a cow's foot?"

—Sí, señor.

—Dígote que es el mejor bocado del mundo, y que no hay faisán que ansí me sepa.

—Pues pruebe, señor, y verá qué tal está.

Póngole en las uñas la otra y tres o cuatro raciones de pan de lo más blanco, y asentóseme al lado y comienza a comer como aquel que lo había gana, royendo cada huesecillo de aquéllos mejor que un galgo suyo lo hiciera.

—Con almodrote —decía— es este singular manjar.

"Con mejor salsa lo comes tú", respondí yo paso.

—Por Dios, que me ha sabido como si hoy no hobiera comido bocado.

"¡Ansí me vengan los buenos años como es ello!", dije yo entre mí.

Pidióme el jarro del agua y díselo como lo había traído. Es señal, que pues no le faltaba el agua, que no le había a mi amo sobrado la comida. Bebimos, y muy contentos nos fuimos a dormir, como la noche pasada.

Y por evitar prolijidad, desta manera estuvimos ocho o diez días, yéndose el pecador en la mañana con aquel contento y paso contado a papar aire por las calles, teniendo en el pobre Lázaro una cabeza de lobo.

Contemplaba yo muchas veces mi desastre, que escapando de los amos ruines que había tenido, y buscando mejoría, viniese a topar con quien no sólo no me mantuviese, mas a quien yo había de mantener. Con todo, le quería bien, con ver que no tenía ni podía más. Y antes le había lástima que enemistad. Y muchas veces, por llevar a la posada con que él lo pasase, yo lo pasaba mal.

Porque una mañana, levantándose el triste en camisa, subió a lo alto de la casa a hacer sus menesteres, y en tanto yo, por salir de sospecha, desenvolvile el jubón y las calzas, que a la cabecera dejó, y hallé una bolsilla de terciopelo raso, hecho cien dobleces y sin maldita la blanca ni señal que la hobiese tenido mucho tiempo. "Este, decía yo, es pobre, y nadie da lo que no tiene; mas el avariento ciego y el malaventurado mezquino clérigo, que, con dárselo Dios a ambos, al uno de mano besada y al otro

"Yes, sir."

"I tell you, that's the finest dish in the world, and I find it tastier than any pheasant."

"Then taste it, sir, and you'll see how good it is."

I placed the foot in his hands,[49] along with three or four portions of bread, from the whitest part; he sat down beside me and began eating like a man with a hearty appetite, gnawing each of the little bones more thoroughly than one of his hunting hounds would.

"This excellent dish," he said, "is made with a garlic and oil sauce."

"You're eating it with a better sauce,"[50] I replied quietly.

"By God, I found it as tasty as if I hadn't eaten a bite today."

"May I have no good years if that isn't the exact truth!" I said to myself.

He asked me for the water jug, which I handed him just as full as when I had brought it. Since he didn't lack water, that was a sign that my master hadn't had lots of food earlier on. We drank and went to bed very contentedly, as on the preceding night.

To make a long story short, we spent eight or ten days that way; every morning that poor sinner would go out, looking contented and walking at a measured pace, to spend his time on the streets doing nothing, since in poor Lázaro he had a goose that laid golden eggs.[51]

I frequently meditated on my unlucky stars: escaping from the terrible masters I had had and seeking a betterment of my lot, I had run into someone who not only didn't support me, but whom I had to support. All the same, I liked him, seeing that that was all he had or could do. I was more sorry for him than hostile to him. And many times, in order to bring home something for him to eat, I went hungry myself.

One morning, when the poor fellow got out of bed in his shirt and went upstairs to answer the call of nature,[52] I, eager to resolve my doubts, unfolded the doublet and breeches he had left at the head of the bed, and I found a small purse of smooth velvet, folded into a hundred folds and containing not a single *blanca* or any sign that it had contained any for a long time. "This man is poor," I said, "and no one can give something he doesn't own. Since the stingy blind man and that damned miserly priest both got sustenance from God, one when people kissed his hand and made an offering, and the other by means

---

49. The Spanish has an untranslatable play on words: "I placed in his *uñas* (fingernails) that other *uña* (the cow's foot). 50. Referring to the proverb "Hunger is the best sauce." 51. Literally: "he had a wolf's head." The killer of a wolf was rewarded when he exhibited its head. 52. Chamberpots were kept in the attic.

de lengua suelta, me mataban de hambre, aquéllos es justo desamar, y aquéste de haber mancilla".

Dios es testigo que hoy día, cuando topo con alguno de su hábito con aquel paso y pompa, le he lástima con pensar si padece lo que aquél le vi sufrir. Al cual, con toda su pobreza, holgaría de servir más que a los otros por lo que he dicho. Sólo tenía dél un poco de descontento: que quisiera yo que no tuviera tanta presunción, mas que abajara un poco su fantasía con lo mucho que subía su necesidad. Mas, según me parece, es regla ya entre ellos usada y guardada: aunque no haya cornado de trueco, ha de andar el birrete en su lugar. El Señor lo remedie, que ya con este mal han de morir.

Pues, estando yo en tal estado, pasando la vida que digo, quiso mi mala fortuna, que de perseguirme no era satisfecha, que en aquella trabajada y vergonzosa vivienda no durase. Y fue, como el año en esta tierra fuese estéril de pan, acordaron el Ayuntamiento que todos los pobres estranjeros se fuesen de la ciudad, con pregón que el que de allí adelante topasen fuese punido con azotes. Y así ejecutando la ley, desde a cuatro días que el pregón se dio, vi llevar una procesión de pobres azotando por las Cuatro Calles. Lo cual me puso tan gran espanto, que nunca osé desmandarme a demandar.

Aquí viera, quien vello pudiera, la abstinencia de mi casa y la tristeza y silencio de los moradores, tanto, que nos acaeció estar dos o tres días sin comer bocado ni hablaba palabra. A mí diéronme la vida unas mujercillas hilanderas de algodón, que hacían bonetes, y vivían par de nosotros, con las cuales yo tuve vecindad y conocimiento. Que de la lacería que les traía me daban alguna cosilla, con la cual muy pasado me pasaba.

Y no tenía tanta lástima de mí como del lastimado de mi amo, que en ocho días maldito el bocado que comió. A lo menos en casa bien lo estuvimos sin comer. No sé yo cómo o dónde andaba y qué comía. ¡Y velle venir a mediodía la calle abajo, con estirado cuerpo, más largo que galgo de buena casta! Y por lo que toca a su negra, que dicen, honra, tomaba una paja, de las que aun asaz no había en casa, y salía a la puerta escarbando los dientes que

of his ready tongue, and they still starved me to death, it's right for me to hate them, whereas I have pity for this man."

God is my witness that today, when I meet someone of his rank walking in the same pompous way, I pity him, wondering if he is suffering the pains that I saw *him* bear so patiently. Poor as he was, I'd rather work for him than for the others, for the reasons I've stated. I was just a little unhappy with him: I would have liked him to be a little less conceited, to lower his presumptuousness to suit the height of his indigence. But it seems to me to be a rule practiced and cherished among his sort: though they don't own the tiniest coin, their cap must remain in its place.[53] May God help them, because they're going to have that sickness till they die.

Well, while my condition was as described and I was leading my life this way, my evil fortune, which wasn't tired of pursuing me, brought it about that I couldn't remain in that difficult and shameful state. It was this way: Since there was a shortage of grain in the region that year, the city council decreed that all paupers from outside should leave town; they announced that any such encountered thenceforth would be flogged. The law went into effect, and, four days after the proclamation, I saw a procession of paupers being led through the Four Streets[54] and flogged. This frightened me so badly that I never again dared let myself go and beg.

Anyone observing us could clearly see at that point in time how bare my house was, and how sad and silent its occupants; so much so, that we had occasion to remain two or three days without eating a bite, and my master said not a word. As for me, I was kept alive by some low-class women who spun cotton and made caps; they lived alongside us, and I had become an acquaintance and good neighbor of theirs. From the pittance they themselves possessed, they gave me a few trifles, on which I just barely got along.[55]

I wasn't as sorry for myself as I was for my wretched master, who ate not a bite for a week. At least, we didn't eat at home for all that time. I don't know how or where he went, or what he ate. And to see him coming down the street at noon with his stiff beanpole of a body, longer than a pedigreed greyhound! And as for his damned honor, as they call it, he used to take a straw—and even those were none too plentiful in our house—and go outside the door, poking it around in

---

53. And not be readily doffed.    54. Between the Cathedral and the main square (Zocodover).    55. The Spanish has a pun on *me pasaba* and *pasado,* which may mean "like a dried fruit."

nada entre sí tenían, quejándose toda vía de aquel mal solar, diciendo:

—Malo está de ver, que la desdicha desta vivienda lo hace. Como ves, es lóbrega, triste, obscura. Mientras aquí estuviéremos hemos de padecer. Ya deseo que se acabe este mes por salir della.

Pues, estando en esta afligida y hambrienta persecución, un día, no sé por cuál dicha o ventura, en el pobre poder de mi amo entró un real, con el cual él vino a casa tan ufano como si tuviera el tesoro de Venecia, y con gesto muy alegre y risueño me lo dio, diciendo:

—Toma, Lázaro, que Dios ya va abriendo su mano. Ve a la plaza y merca pan y vino y carne: ¡quebremos el ojo al diablo! Y más te hago saber porque te huelgues: que he alquilado otra casa, y en ésta desastrada no hemos de estar más de en cumpliendo el mes. ¡Maldita sea ella y el que en ella puso la primera teja, que con mal en ella entré! Por Nuestro Señor, cuanto ha que en ella vivo, gota de vino ni bocado de carne no he comido, ni he habido descanso ninguno; ¡mas tal vista tiene y tal obscuridad y tristeza! Ve y ven presto, y comamos hoy como condes.

Tomo mi real y jarro, y a los pies dándoles priesa, comienzo a subir mi calle, encaminando mis pasos para la plaza, muy contento y alegre. Mas ¿qué me aprovecha si está constituido en mi triste fortuna que ningún gozo me venga sin zozobra? Y ansí fue éste, porque yendo la calle arriba, echando mi cuenta en lo que le emplearía que fuese mejor y más provechosamente gastado, dando infinitas gracias a Dios que a mi amo había hecho con dinero, a deshora me vino al encuentro un muerto que por la calle abajo muchos clérigos y gente en unas andas traían.

Arriméme a la pared por darles lugar, y desque el cuerpo pasó, venían luego a par del lecho una que debía ser mujer del difunto, cargada de luto, y con ella otras muchas mujeres, la cual iba llorando a grandes voces y diciendo:

—Marido y señor mío: ¿adónde os me llevan? ¡A la casa triste y desdichada, a la casa lóbrega y obscura, a la casa donde nunca comen ni beben!

Yo, que aquello oí, juntóseme el cielo con la tierra y dije: "¡Oh, desdichado de mí! ¡Para mi casa llevan este muerto!".

his teeth, which had nothing between them, constantly complaining about that unlucky building site, as follows:

"Things are bad, and this unfortunate house is to blame. As you see, it's gloomy, dismal, dark. As long as we remain here, we've got to suffer. I wish this month were already over so we could leave."

Well, while we were afflicted by this terrible hunger spell, one day, I don't know through what good luck or chance, a *real* fell into my master's poor hands; he came home with the coin as proud as if he owned the Venetian treasury, and gave it to me with a very happy, smiling face, saying:

"Here, Lázaro, God is now opening His hand for us. Go to the market and buy bread, wine, and meat: we'll put the Devil's eye out! And I have some other news to make you happy: I've rented another house, and we don't have to stay in this ill-starred one after the month is up. A curse on it, and on the man who laid the first tile on it, because it was an evil day when I set foot in it! By Our Lord, the whole time I've been living here, I haven't tasted a drop of wine or a bite of meat, or had any proper rest, it's so ugly, and so dark and dismal! Go and come back right away, and let's eat like counts today."

I took the *real* and the jug, and, as fast as I could go, I started to head up the street, in the direction of the market, very pleased and happy. But what's the good, if my bad luck is so constituted that I can't have any pleasure without its being upset? And so it was that time, because, as I went up the street, planning on how to spend the money best and most advantageously, and thanking God a thousand times for supplying my master with money, all at once I saw coming my way a dead man whom many priests and other people were carrying down the street on a bier.

I hugged the wall to give them room, and, after the body passed by, there came right after the bier a woman who must have been the dead man's wife, dressed in mourning and accompanied by many other women. She was weeping loudly as she went and saying:

"My husband and master, where are they taking you? To the dismal, unlucky house, to the gloomy, dark house, to the house where no one ever eats or drinks!"

Hearing those words, I became thoroughly alarmed[56] and said: "How unfortunate I am! They're taking this dead man to my house!"[57]

---

56. Literally: "the sky was joined to the earth for me." 57. According to at least one commentator, the inclusion here of this time-honored joke was the author's worst mistake. It doesn't fit the character of Lázaro, who isn't timid or superstitious, and who has seen many corpses at funerals.

Dejo el camino que llevaba y hendí por medio de la gente, y vuelvo por la calle abajo, a todo el más correr que pude, para mi casa; y entrado en ella, cierro a grande priesa, invocando el auxilio y favor de mi amo, abrazándome dél, que me venga ayudar y a defender la entrada. El cual, algo alterado, pensando que fuese otra cosa, me dijo: —¿Qué es eso, mozo? ¿Qué voces das? ¿Qué has? ¿Por qué cierras la puerta con tal furia?

—¡Oh, señor —dije yo—, acuda aquí, que nos traen acá un muerto!

—¿Cómo así? —respondió él.

—Aquí arriba lo encontré, y venía diciendo su mujer: "¡Marido y señor mío! ¿Adónde os llevan? ¡A la casa lóbrega y obscura, a la casa triste y desdichada, a la casa donde nunca comen ni beben!". Acá, señor, nos le traen.

Y, ciertamente, cuando mi amo esto oyó, aunque no tenía por qué estar muy risueño, rió tanto, que muy gran rato estuvo sin poder hablar. En este tiempo tenía ya yo echada la aldaba a la puerta y puesto el hombro en ella por más defensa. Pasó la gente con su muerto, y yo todavía me recelaba que nos le habían de meter en casa. Y desque fue ya más harto de reír que de comer el bueno de mi amo, díjome:

—Verdad es, Lázaro; según la viuda lo va diciendo, tú tuviste razón de pensar lo que pensaste; mas, pues Dios lo ha hecho mejor y pasan adelante, abre, abre y ve por de comer.

—Déjalos, señor, acaben de pasar la calle —dije yo. Al fin vino mi amo a la puerta de la calle y ábrela esforzándome, que bien era menester, según el miedo y alteración, y me torno a encaminar. Mas aunque comimos bien aquel día, maldito el gusto yo tomaba en ello, ni en aquellos tres días torné en mi color; y mi amo muy risueño todas las veces que se le acordaba aquella mi consideración.

De esta manera estuve con mi tercero y pobre amo, que fue este escudero, algunos días, y en todos deseando saber la intención de su venida y estada en esta tierra, porque, desde el primer día que con él asenté, le conocí ser estranjero, por el poco conocimiento y trato que con los naturales della tenía. Al fin se cumplió mi deseo, y supe lo que deseaba, porque un día que habíamos comido razonablemente y estaba algo contento, contóme su hacienda, y díjome ser de Castilla la Vieja y que había dejado su tierra no más de por no quitar el bonete a un caballero su vecino.

I abandoned my line of march, cut through the crowd, and went back down the street toward home as fast as I could run. Once inside, I locked the door in great haste, calling on my master to save and help me; clasping him around, I begged him to come and help me keep them from coming in. He, a little upset because he thought it was something else, said: "What's this, boy? Why are you yelling? What's wrong with you? Why are you locking the door in such a frenzy?"

"Oh, master," I said, "come here and help, because they're bringing a dead man here!"

"How's that?" he replied.

"I ran across him up the street, and his wife was saying: 'My husband and master, where are they taking you? To the gloomy, dark house, to the sad, unlucky house, to the house where no one ever eats or drinks!' Sir, it must be here that they're bringing him!"

And, truly, when my master heard that, even though he didn't have much to laugh about, he laughed so hard that he couldn't talk for some time. Meanwhile I had fastened the door latch and set my shoulder against the door for greater protection. The people passed by with their corpse, but I was still afraid they would put it in our house. After my good master had had more of his fill of laughter than of food, he said:

"It's true, Lázaro; from what the widow said, you were right to think what you did; but, since God has saved us and they're passing by, open the door, open and go buy food."

"Sir, let them keep on; let them go all the way down the street," I said. At last my master came up to the street door and made me open it, which I really needed, I was so frightened and upset; and I went off on my way again. But, even though we dined well that day, I couldn't find any taste in the food, and I didn't get my color back for three days afterward. My master burst out laughing every time he remembered those reflections of mine.

I went on living that way with my poor third master, this nobleman, for several days, constantly eager to find out why he had come to this city and was dwelling here, since, from the first day I entered his service, I knew he was a stranger because he was so unfamiliar with things and mingled so little with the locals. Finally my wishes were granted and I learned what I wanted to know, because one day, after we had dined moderately well and he felt a bit contented, he told me about his affairs. He said he was from Old Castile, and that he had left his hometown solely to avoid doffing his hat to a knight who was his neighbor.

—Señor —dije yo—, si él era lo que decís y tenía más que vos, ¿no errábades en no quitárselo primero, pues decís que él también os lo quitaba?

—Sí es, y sí tiene, y también me lo quitaba él a mí; mas, de cuantas veces yo se le quitaba primero, no fuera malo comedirse él alguna y ganarme por la mano.

—Paréceme, señor —le dije yo—, que en eso no mirara, mayormente con mis mayores que yo y que tienen más.

—Eres mochacho —me respondió— y no sientes las cosas de la honra, en que el día de hoy está todo el caudal de los hombres de bien. Pues te hago saber que yo soy, como ves, un escudero; mas, ¡vótote a Dios!, si al conde topo en la calle y no me quita muy bien quitado del todo el bonete, que otra vez que venga me sepa yo entrar en una casa, fingiendo yo en ella algún negocio, o atravesar otra calle, si la hay, antes que llegue a mí, por no quitárselo. Que un hidalgo no debe a otro que a Dios y al rey nada, ni es justo, siendo hombre de bien, se descuide un punto de tener en mucho su persona. Acuérdome que un día deshonré en mi tierra a un oficial, y quise ponerle las manos, porque cada vez que le topaba, me decía: "Mantenga Dios a Vuestra Merced." "Vos, don villano ruin — le dije yo—, ¿por qué no sois bien criado? ¿Manténgaos Dios, me habéis de decir, como si fuese quienquiera?" De allí adelante, de aquí acullá me quitaba el bonete, y hablaba como debía.

—¿Y no es buena maña de saludar un hombre a otro —dije yo— decirle que le mantenga Dios?

—¡Mira mucho de enhoramala! —dijo él—. A los hombres de poca arte dicen eso; mas a los más altos, como yo, no les han de hablar menos de: "Beso las manos de Vuestra Merced", o por lo menos: "Bésoos, señor, las manos", si el que me habla es caballero. Y ansí, de aquel de mi tierra que me atestaba de mantenimiento nunca más le quise sufrir, ni sufriría, ni sufriré a hombre del mundo, de el rey abajo, que "Manténgaos Dios" me diga.

"Pecador de mí —dije yo—, por eso tiene tan poco cuidado de mantenerte, pues no sufres que nadie se lo ruegue."

—Mayormente —dijo— que no soy tan pobre que no tengo en mi tierra un solar de casas, que a estar ellas en pie y bien

"Sir," I said, "if he was of the rank that you state, and if he was richer than you, weren't you wrong not to take off your hat first, since you say he also took off his hat to you?"

"He *is* of that rank, and he *is* richer, and he *did* also doff his hat to me; but, after all those times when I doffed mine first, he wouldn't have done wrong to venture just one time to anticipate me."

"It seems to me, sir," I said, "that I wouldn't have let that bother me, especially with people who outrank me and are wealthier."

"You're a boy," he replied, "and you can't have the proper feeling for affairs of honor, which nowadays represents all the riches of a gentleman. Let me tell you that I am a squire in rank, of the lower nobility, as you see; but, I swear to God, if I meet a count in the street and he doesn't raise his hat to me, high and all the way off his head, the next time I see him coming I'll walk into a house, pretending I have some business there, or cross over to another street, if there is one, before he comes up to me, to avoid doffing mine. For a nobleman owes nothing to anyone but God and the King, and it's wrong for a gentleman to derogate a jot from his self-respect. I remember that one day back home I insulted an artisan, and wanted to lay hands on him, because every time I met him, he'd say: 'May God sustain you, Your Honor.' 'You, you miserable peasant,' I replied that day, 'why aren't you polite? Must you say "May God sustain you" to me, as if I were just anybody?' From then on without fail, he doffed his hat to me and addressed me properly."

"And isn't it a proper way for one man to greet another," I asked, "when he wishes that God will sustain you?"

"I should say not!" he replied. "That's said to men of low rank, but to those of more elevated rank, like myself, the least that should be said is 'I kiss Your Honor's hands,' or, at the very least, 'Sir, I kiss your hands,' if the man addressing me is a knight. And so, I never again wanted to put up with that fellow back home who crammed me full of sustain-you's; nor would I put up with it; nor will I allow anyone in the world, from the King on down, to say 'May God sustain you' to me."

"Sinner that I am," I said to myself, "that's why He's so little concerned about sustaining you, because you won't allow anyone to pray to Him for that purpose."

"Especially," he continued, "because I'm not so poor that I don't possess a building site back home, which, if built upon with good, solid

labradas, diez y seis leguas de donde nací, en aquella
Costanilla de Valladolid, valdrían más de docientas veces mil
maravedís, según se podrían hacer grandes y buenas; y tengo
un palomar, que a no estar derribado como está, daría cada
año más de docientos palominos; y otras cosas que me callo,
que dejé por lo que tocaba a mi honra. Y vine a esta ciudad
pensando que hallaría un buen asiento, mas no me ha sucedido como pensé. Canónigos y señores de la iglesia muchos
hallo, mas es gente tan limitada, que no los sacarán de su paso
todo el mundo. Caballeros de media talla también me ruegan;
mas servir con éstos es gran trabajo, porque de hombre os
habéis de convertir en malilla, y si no, "Andá con Dios" os
dicen. Y las más veces son los pagamentos a largos plazos, y las
más y las más ciertas comido por servido. Ya cuando quieren
reformar conciencia y satisfaceros vuestros sudores, sois libra-
dos en la recámara, en un sudado jubón, o raída capa o sayo.
Ya cuando asienta un hombre con un señor de título, todavía
pasa su laceria. ¿Pues, por ventura, no hay en mí habilidad
para servir y contentar a éstos? Por Dios, si con él topase, muy
gran su privado pienso que fuese, y que mil servicios le hiciese, porque yo sabría mentille tan bien como otro, y
agradalle a las mil maravillas; reille hía mucho sus donaires y
costumbres, aunque no fuesen las mejores del mundo; nunca
decirle cosa con que le pesase, aunque mucho le cumpliese;
ser muy diligente en su persona, en dicho y hecho; no me
matar por no hacer bien las cosas que él no había de ver; y
ponerme a reñir donde lo oyese con la gente de servicio,
porque pareciese tener gran cuidado de lo que a él tocaba; si
riñese con algún su criado, dar unos puntillos agudos para le
encender la ira, y que pareciesen en favor de el culpado; decirle bien de lo que bien le estuviese, y por el contrario, ser
malicioso, mofador, malsinar a los de casa y a los de fuera;
pesquisar y procurar de saber vidas ajenas para contárselas,
y otras muchas galas desta calidad, que hoy día se usan en

houses and relocated on the Costanilla in Valladolid,[58] sixteen leagues from my birthplace, would be worth two hundred thousand *maravedís,* depending on how big and fine the houses were. I also possess a dovecote,[59] which, if it weren't a wreck as it now is, would produce over two hundred young pigeons yearly; and there are other things I won't mention, all of which I abandoned to protect my honor. And I came to this city thinking I'd find some suitable employment here,[60] but it hasn't turned out as I wished. I find plenty of cathedral canons and great churchmen, but they're such ungenerous people that no one can get them to change their ways. I've also had offers from knights of middling quality, but serving them is a great chore, because you have to change yourself from a man into a wild card,[61] or else they tell you good-bye. And very often your salary only falls due at long intervals, but most of the time you can rely on receiving only room and board. When they want to square their conscience and repay you for your labors, your account is settled in the wardrobe with a sweaty doublet or a threadbare cloak or tunic. Even when a man enters the service of a titled nobleman, he still has to put up with misery. Now, don't you think I'm clever enough to serve such people and give satisfaction? By God, if I came across one, I think I'd make a fine confidential servant and I'd perform a thousand services for him, because I'd know how to lie to him as well as anyone else could, and please him wonderfully well. I'd laugh heartily at his jokes and admire his habits, even if they weren't the best in the world. I'd never say anything that would annoy him, however much he might deserve it. In his presence I'd be extremely diligent in word and deed. I wouldn't knock myself out doing things properly if he wasn't liable to notice them. I'd start quarrels with his lower servants if he was around to hear, so that I'd seem to be greatly concerned for his affairs. If he quarreled with a servant, I'd get in some digs[62] to inflame his anger, making remarks that seemed to favor the guilty party. I'd say good things about what he considered good, and, on the other hand, I'd be malicious and scornful, and I'd inform on those inside the house and out. I'd investigate and try to learn about other people's doings so I could report them to him; and many other delightful actions of that sort

58. Valladolid harbored the royal court from 1543 to 1559, and enjoyed a real-estate boom around the time when the novel was published. The reference here is thus a strong point in favor of those who believe that the date of composition, and the time of the action, were not very long before the editions of 1554. The Costanilla was the most fashionable street in town.    59. This was a privilege of the clergy and nobility; pigeon raising could be profitable.    60. A nobleman could only work for someone of higher status, in some position of honor.    61. That is, adapt your own nature to anything they want you to do.    62. Or: "raise my voice."

palacio y a los señores dél parecen bien. Y no quieren ver en
sus casas hombres virtuosos; antes los aborrecen y tienen en
poco y llaman necios, y que no son personas de negocios ni
con quien el señor se puede descuidar; y con éstos los astutos
usan, como digo, el día de hoy, de lo que yo usaría; mas no
quiere mi ventura que le halle.

Desta manera lamentaba también su adversa fortuna mi amo,
dándome relación de su persona valerosa.

Pues estando en esto, entró por la puerta un hombre y una
vieja. El hombre le pide el alquiler de la casa y la vieja el de la
cama. Hacen cuenta, y de dos en dos meses le alcanzaron lo que
él en un año no alcanzara. Pienso que fueron doce o trece reales.
Y él les dio muy buena respuesta: que saldría a la plaza a trocar
una pieza de a dos y que a la tarde volviesen; mas su salida fue
sin vuelta.

Por manera que a la tarde ellos volvieron; mas fue tarde. Yo
les dije que aún no era venido. Venida la noche y él no, yo hube
miedo de quedar en casa solo, y fuime a las vecinas y contéles el
caso, y allí dormí.

Venida la mañana, los acreedores vuelven y preguntan por el
vecino, mas a estotra puerta. Las mujeres le responden: —Veis
aquí su mozo y la llave de la puerta.

Ellos me preguntaron por él, y díjele que no sabía adónde estaba y que tampoco había vuelto a casa desde que salió a trocar
la pieza, y que pensaba que de mí y de ellos se había ido con el
trueco.

De que esto me oyeron, van por un alguacil y un escribano. Y
helos do vuelven luego con ellos, y toman la llave, y llámanme, y
llaman testigos, y abren la puerta, y entran a embargar la hacienda de mi amo hasta ser pagados de su deuda. Anduvieron
toda la casa, y halláronla desembarazada, como he contado, y dí-
cenme: —¿Qué es de la hacienda de tu amo: sus arcas y paños
de pared y alhajas de casa?

—No sé yo eso —le respondí.

—Sin duda —dicen ellos— esta noche lo deben de haber
alzado y llevado a alguna parte. Señor alguacil, prended a este
mozo, que él sabe dónde está.

En esto vino el alguacil y echóme mano por el collar del

which are customary in palaces nowadays and find favor with their owners. They don't want to see virtuous men in their homes; in fact, they loathe them, look down on them, and call them fools, people unfit to deal with, people the master can't feel safe with. And, as I've said, shrewd people nowadays handle such masters the way I would; but my bad luck won't allow me to find one."

In such manner my master, too, bewailed his adverse fortunes, giving me an account of his valiant character.

Well, while we were engaged in this conversation, a man and an old woman came in at the door. The man asked him for the house rent, and the woman for the rent on the bed. They toted up their accounts, and for a two-month period they arrived at a sum that my master wouldn't have managed to accumulate in a year. I think it was twelve or thirteen *reales*. He answered them very cordially: he would go to the market and break a two-*castellano* coin,[63] and they should come back in the afternoon. But when he left, it was never to return.

And so, they came back later, in the afternoon, but later was too late. I told them he wasn't back yet. When night came and he didn't, I was afraid of staying in the house alone. I went to the women next door, told them what had happened, and slept there.

The next morning, the creditors came and asked the women about their neighbor, but got little satisfaction.[64] The women told them: "This is his servant boy, and here is the key to the door."

The creditors asked me about him, and I told them I didn't know where he was, that he hadn't come home since he had gone out to break the coin, and that I thought he had abandoned both me and them with that money-changing.

When they heard me say that, they went to fetch a constable and a clerk. They came back with them at once, took the key, called me, called witnesses, opened the door, and went in to seize my master's belongings until their debt was paid. They went all through the house. Finding it as bare as I've described, they said to me: "What about your master's belongings: his chests, wall hangings, and furniture?"

"I have no idea," I replied.

"No doubt," they said, "they must have removed them last night and taken them somewhere else. Constable, arrest this boy, because he knows where his master is."

Thereupon the constable came and seized the collar of my doublet,

---

63. A gold coin worth about 30 *reales*.    64. Literally: "[go] to the other door [because this one doesn't open]."

jubón, diciendo: —Mochacho, tú eres preso si no descubres los bienes deste tu amo.

Yo, como en otra tal no me hubiese visto (porque asido del collar sí había sido muchas y infinitas veces, mas era mansamente dél trabado, para que mostrase el camino al que no vía), yo hube mucho miedo, y, llorando, prometíle de decir lo que preguntaban.

—Bien está —dicen ellos—. Pues di todo lo que sabes y no hayas temor.—Sentóse el escribano en un poyo para escrebir el inventario, preguntándome qué tenía.

—Señores —dije yo—, lo que éste mi amo tiene, según él me dijo, es un muy buen solar de casas y un palomar derribado.

—Bien está —dicen ellos—; por poco que eso valga, hay para nos entregar de la deuda. ¿Y a qué parte de la ciudad tiene eso? —me preguntaron.

—En su tierra —les respondí.

—Por Dios, que está bueno el negocio —dijeron ellos—, ¿y adónde es su tierra?

—De Castilla la Vieja me dijo él que era —le dije yo.

Riéronse mucho el alguacil y el escribano, diciendo: —Bastante relación es ésta para cobrar vuestra deuda, aunque mejor fuese.

Las vecinas, que estaban presentes, dijeron: —Señores, éste es un niño inocente y ha pocos días que está con ese escudero, y no sabe dél más que vuestras mercedes, sino cuanto el pecadorcico se llega aquí a nuestra casa, y le damos de comer lo que podemos por amor de Dios, y a las noches se iba a dormir con él.

Vista mi inocencia, dejáronme, dándome por libre. Y el alguacil y el escribano piden al hombre y a la mujer sus derechos. Sobre lo cual tuvieron gran contienda y ruido. Porque ellos alegaron no ser obligados a pagar, pues no había de qué ni se hacía el embargo. Los otros decían que habían dejado de ir a otro negocio que les importaba más por venir a aquél.

Finalmente, después de dadas muchas voces, al cabo carga un porquerón con el viejo alfamar de la vieja, aunque no iba muy cargado. Allá van todos cinco dando voces. No sé en qué paró: creo yo que el pecador alfamar pagara por todos. Y bien se empleaba, pues el tiempo que había de reposar y descansar de los trabajos pasados se andaba alquilando.

Así, como he contado, me dejó mi pobre tercero amo, do acabé de conocer mi ruin dicha, pues, señalándose todo lo que

saying: "Boy, you're under arrest if you don't tell us where your master's property is."

Since I had never found myself in a similar situation (I had been grabbed by the collar time and time again, but gently, so that I might show the way to the blind man), I was severely frightened. I started to cry and promised to tell them what they wanted to know.

"Good!" they said. "Then, tell all you know and don't be afraid." The clerk sat down on a stone bench to make out the inventory; he asked me what my master owned.

"Gentlemen," I said, "according to what he told me, what my master owns is a very good building site and a wrecked dovecote."

"Good!" they said. "No matter how little that's worth, it will help compensate us for the debt. And what part of town is that in?" they asked.

"In his hometown," I replied.

"By God, what a good deal this is!" they said. "And where is his hometown?"

"He said it was in Old Castile," I replied.

The constable and clerk laughed heartily, saying: "This report makes it certain that you'll recover your debt, even if it were bigger."

The women from next door, who were present, said: "Gentlemen, he's an innocent child and has been with this nobleman only a few days. He knows no more about him than Your Honors do. In fact, the poor little beggar has been coming over to our house, and we've been feeding him whatever we can out of charity. At night he went back to sleep in his master's house."

In view of my innocence, they released me, declaring I was free. Then the constable and clerk asked the man and woman for their fee. Over this there was a great wrangle and racket. The debtors affirmed that they had no obligation to pay because nothing had been accomplished and no property had been seized. The others said that they had neglected answering another call that would have been more profitable, when they answered this one.

In short, after a lot of shouting, an assistant constable finally carried away the old lady's old blanket, though it was no strain on him. All five of them departed, shouting. I don't know how it ended up, but I think that that sinful blanket bore everybody's costs. And it deserved to do so, because at its age, when it should have retired and rested from its past labors, it was still hiring itself out.

In the manner I have related, my poor third master abandoned me. In this I became fully aware of my terrible luck, which, making its

podría contra mí, hacía mis negocios tan al revés, que los amos, que suelen ser dejados de los mozos, en mí no fuese ansí, mas que mi amo me dejase y huyese de mí.

## TRATADO CUARTO

### Cómo Lázaro se asentó con un fraile de la Merced y de lo que le acaeció con él

Hube de buscar el cuarto, y éste fue un fraile de la Merced, que las mujercillas que digo me encaminaron. Al cual ellas le llamaban pariente. Gran enemigo del coro y de comer en el convento, perdido por andar fuera, amicísimo de negocios seglares y visitar. Tanto, que pienso que rompía él más zapatos que todo el convento. Este me dio los primeros zapatos que rompí en mi vida; mas no me duraron ocho días, ni yo pude con su trote durar más. Y por esto, y por otras cosillas que no digo salí dél.

## TRATADO QUINTO

### Cómo Lázaro se asentó con un buldero y de las cosas que con él pasó

En el quinto por mi ventura di, que fue un buldero, el más de-senvuelto y desvergonzado, y el mayor echador dellas que jamás yo vi ni ver espero, ni pienso que nadie vio. Porque tenía y bus-caba modos y maneras y muy sotiles invenciones.

En entrando en los lugares do habían de presentar la bula, primero presentaba a los clérigos o curas algunas cosillas, no tampoco de mucho valor ni substancia: una lechuga murciana, si era por el tiempo; un par de limas o naranjas; un melocotón; un par de duraznos; cada sendas peras verdiniales. Ansí procuraba

hostility to me crystal clear, turned all my doings so upside-down that, whereas masters generally are left by their servants, for me it wasn't so, but my master abandoned and ran away from me.

## CHAPTER FOUR

### How Lázaro Was Employed by a Mercedarian Friar, and What Happened to Him in His Company

I had to look for a fourth master, and this proved to be a Mercedarian friar,[65] to whom the low-class women I have mentioned directed me. They said he was a relative.[66] He was a great enemy of prayers in the choir and meals in the refectory, but was hell-bent on wandering abroad, being extremely fond of secular matters and paying visits. So much so, that I think he wore out more shoes than anyone else in the monastery. He gave me the first shoes I ever wore out in my life; but they didn't last me a week, and I couldn't keep up with his gadding about. For that reason, and for a few other trifling matters that I won't mention,[67] I left him.

## CHAPTER FIVE

### How Lázaro Was Employed by an Indulgence Seller, and of the Things That Befell Him in His Company

The fifth master I chanced to fall in with was a seller of indulgences,[68] the most brazen and shameless, and the most skillful dispatcher of them, that I've ever seen or hope to see: that anyone has ever seen, I think. Because he knew and sought out special ways and means to unload them, including some very subtle contrivances.

On arriving in places where they were going to promote the indulgence, first he presented to the priests or curates some little things, not of much value or substance, either: a lettuce from Murcia, if the season was right; a pair of limes or oranges; a large peach or a couple

---

65. See the section "The Characters" in the Introduction.   66. An indication of illicit relations.   67. Many commentators are convinced that this means the friar abused Lázaro sexually.   68. See "The Characters" in the Introduction.

tenerlos propicios, porque favoreciesen su negocio y llamasen sus feligreses a tomar la bula.

Ofreciéndosele a él las gracias, informábase de la suficiencia dellos. Si decían que entendían, no hablaba en latín, por no dar tropezón; mas aprovechábase de un gentil y bien cortado romance y desenvoltísima lengua. Y si sabían que los dichos clérigos eran de los reverendos (digo, que más con dineros que con letras, y con reverendas se ordenan), hacíase entre ellos un santo Tomás y hablaba dos horas en latín. A lo menos, que lo parecía, aunque no lo era.

Cuando por bien no le tomaban las bulas, buscaba cómo por mal se las tomasen. Y para aquello hacía molestias al pueblo, e otras veces con mañosos artificios. Y porque todos los que le veía hacer sería largo de contar, diré uno muy sotil y donoso, con el cual probaré bien su suficiencia.

En un lugar de la Sagra de Toledo había predicado dos o tres días, haciendo sus acostumbradas diligencias, y no le habían tomado bula, ni a mi ver tenían intención de se la tomar. Estaba dado al diablo con aquello, y pensando qué hacer, se acordó de convidar al pueblo para otro día de mañana despedir la bula.

Y esa noche, después de cenar, pusiéronse a jugar la colación él y el alguacil. Y sobre el juego vinieron a reñir y a haber malas palabras. El llamó al alguacil ladrón, y el otro a él falsario. Sobre esto, el señor comisario, mi señor, tomó un lanzón que en el portal do jugaban estaba. El alguacil puso mano a su espada, que en la cinta tenía.

Al ruido y voces que todos dimos, acuden los huéspedes y vecinos, y métense en medio. Y ellos, muy enojados, procurándose de desembarazar de los que en medio estaban para se matar. Mas como la gente al gran ruido cargase, y la casa estuviese llena della, viendo que no podían afrentarse con las armas, decíanse palabras injuriosas, entre las cuales el alguacil dijo a mi amo que era falsario y las bulas que predicaba que eran falsas.

of smaller peaches; a green pear[69] apiece. Thus he tried to win their favor for his business and get them to urge the faithful to buy an indulgence.

When they came to thank him, he would find out how qualified they were. If they said they understood Latin, he didn't speak it, to avoid making a blunder; instead, he used a smooth, elegant Spanish, which flowed from his tongue. If he saw that these priests were "reverend" (that is, money rather than learning had gained them their position, with letters beginning "Reverend sir"),[70] then among them he turned into a Saint Thomas and spoke in Latin for two hours—at least, what seemed to be Latin, though it wasn't.

When people didn't buy his indulgences readily, he sought ways to get them to do it. To that end, he made trouble for the people, and other times he used crafty tricks. And, since it would take me too long to narrate all the tricks I saw him play, I'll tell you one very sly and funny one, with which I'll fully prove his skill.

In a village in the Sagra de Toledo[71] he had been preaching for two or three days, taking his usual preliminary measures, but the people hadn't bought one indulgence, nor did they intend to, as far as I could see. He was furious over this; planning his course of action, he decided to summon the villagers to appear at the closing ceremony the next morning.

That night after supper, he and his constable gambled to see who would pay for the snack they would have with their wine. They started to quarrel over the game and to insult each other. He called the constable a thief, and the other man called him a counterfeiter. Thereupon the indulgence commissioner, my master, picked up a large lance that was in the hallway where they were gambling. The constable laid hand on his sword, which hung from his belt.

At the noise and shouts we all uttered, our hosts and neighbors came running and intervened. The two combatants, very irritated, tried to shake off those who stood in the way of their killing each other. But since the people crowded around at that great racket, and the inn was full of them, they saw that they couldn't settle accounts with weapons and started insulting each other; among other insults, the constable called my master a counterfeiter and said that the indulgences he preached were fakes.

---

69. Green-colored even when ripe.    70. Letters from a bishop giving another prelate permission to ordain a man who fell under the letter-writer's jurisdiction.    71. A region northeast of Toledo, on the way to Madrid.

Finalmente, que los del pueblo, viendo que no bastaban a ponellos en paz, acordaron de llevar el alguacil de la posada a otra parte. Y así quedó mi amo muy enojado. Y después que los huéspedes y vecinos le hubieron rogado que perdiese el enojo, y se fuese a dormir, se fue, y así nos echamos todos.

La mañana venida, mi amo se fue a la iglesia y mandó tañer a misa y al sermón para despedir la bula. Y el pueblo se juntó, el cual andaba murmurando de las bulas, diciendo cómo eran falsas y que el mesmo alguacil, riñendo, lo había descubierto. De manera que, tras que tenían mala gana de tomalla, con aquello del todo la aborrecieron.

El señor comisario se subió al púlpito, y comienza su sermón, y a animar la gente a que no quedasen sin tanto bien y indulgencia como la santa bula traía. Estando en lo mejor del sermón, entra por la puerta de la iglesia el alguacil, y desque hizo oración, levantóse, y con voz alta y pausada, cuerdamente comenzó a decir:

—Buenos hombres, oídme una palabra, que después oiréis a quien quisiéredes. Yo vine aquí con este echacuervo que os predica, el cual me engañó, y dijo que le favoreciese en este negocio, y que partiríamos la ganancia. Y agora, visto el daño que haría a mi conciencia y a vuestras haciendas, arrepentido de lo hecho, os declaro claramente que las bulas que predica son falsas y que no le creáis ni las toméis, y que yo, *directe* ni *indirecte,* no soy parte en ellas, y que desde agora dejo la vara y doy con ella en el suelo. Y si en algún tiempo éste fuere castigado por la falsedad, que vosotros me seáis testigos cómo yo no soy con él ni le doy a ello ayuda, antes os desengaño y declaro su maldad. —Y acabó su razonamiento.

Algunos hombres honrados que allí estaban se quisieron levantar y echar el alguacil fuera de la iglesia, por evitar escándalo. Mas mi amo les fue a la mano y mandó a todos que, so pena de excomunión, no le estorbasen, mas que le dejasen decir todo lo que quisiese. Y ansí él también tuvo silencio mientras el alguacil dijo todo lo que he dicho. Como calló, mi amo le preguntó si quería decir más, que lo dijese.

El alguacil dijo: —Harto hay más que decir de vos y de vuestra falsedad; mas por agora basta.

El señor comisario se hincó de rodillas en el púlpito, y puestas las manos y mirando al cielo, dijo ansí: —Señor Dios, a quien ninguna cosa es escondida, antes todas manifiestas, y a quien

Finally the villagers, finding themselves insufficient to reconcile them, decided to remove the constable from the inn and take him elsewhere. And thus my master remained there, quite vexed. After our hosts and neighbors begged him to relinquish his anger and go to bed, he did so, and so we all did.

When morning came, my master went to the church and ordered them to ring for Mass and for the concluding indulgence sermon. The villagers gathered, grumbling about the indulgences and saying they were fakes, as the constable himself had revealed during the quarrel. And so, having shown little inclination to buy them previously, now they despised them altogether.

The commissioner ascended the pulpit and began his sermon, urging the people not to neglect all the benefits and pardons that the holy indulgence afforded. When he was at the height of his sermon, the constable came in through the church door; after reciting a prayer, he stood up and, in a loud, calm voice, started to speak quite rationally:

"Good people, allow me to say a word, and then you can listen to whom you choose. I came here in the company of this charlatan who is preaching to you, and who deceived me, asking me to help him out in this deal, and saying we would share the profits. Now, seeing the harm I would do to my conscience and to your pocketbooks, I repent what I have done, and I declare straight out that the indulgences he is preaching are fakes. Don't believe him and don't buy any. I have no part in them, either directly or indirectly, and from here on I put aside my staff of office and throw it to the ground. If at some future time he is punished for his counterfeiting, I want you to be witnesses that I am not part of his entourage and am not aiding him in any way; on the contrary, I'm opening your eyes to his wickedness." And he ended his speech.

A few honorable men among those present wanted to get up and throw the constable out of the church, to avoid a scandal. But my master prevented them; he ordered everyone, under pain of excommunication, not to disturb him, but to let him say all that he wanted. And so, he, too, kept silence while the constable said all that I have reported. When he fell silent, my master asked him to go on with anything more he might have to say.

The constable said: "I have plenty more to say about you and your deceptions, but that's enough for now."

The commissioner fell to his knees in the pulpit; clasping his hands together and looking up to heaven, he said: "My Lord God, to whom nothing is hidden, but all things are revealed, and to whom nothing is

nada es imposible, antes todo posible: tú sabes la verdad y cuán injustamente yo soy afrentado. En lo que a mí toca, yo lo perdono, porque tú, Señor, me perdones. No mires a aquel que no sabe lo que hace ni dice; mas la injuria a ti hecha te suplico, y por justicia te pido, no disimules; porque alguno que está aquí, que por ventura pensó tomar aquesta santa bula, dando crédito a las falsas palabras de aquel hombre lo dejará de hacer, y, pues es tanto perjuicio del prójimo, te suplico yo, Señor, no lo disimules, mas luego muestra aquí milagro, y sea desta manera: que si es verdad lo que aquél dice y que yo traigo maldad y falsedad, este púlpito se hunda comigo y meta siete estados debajo de tierra, do él ni yo jamás parezcamos; y si es verdad lo que yo digo y aquél, persuadido del demonio (por quitar y privar a los que están presentes de tan gran bien), dice maldad, también sea castigado y de todos conocida su malicia.

Apenas había acabado su oración el devoto señor mío, cuando el negro alguacil cae de su estado, y da tan gran golpe en el suelo, que la iglesia toda hizo resonar, y comenzó a bramar y echar espumajos por la boca y torcella y hacer visajes con el gesto, dando de pie y de mano, revolviéndose por aquel suelo a una parte y a otra.

El estruendo y voces de la gente era tan grande, que no se oían unos a otros. Algunos estaban espantados y temerosos. Unos decían: "El Señor le socorra y valga." Otros: "Bien se le emplea, pues levantaba tan falso testimonio."

Finalmente, algunos que allí estaban, y a mi parecer no sin harto temor, se llegaron y le trabaron de los brazos, con los cuales daba fuertes puñadas a los que cerca dél estaban. Otros le tiraban por las piernas, y tuvieron reciamente, porque no había mula falsa en el mundo que tan recias coces tirase. Y así le tuvieron un gran rato, porque más de quince hombres estaban sobre él, y a todos daba las manos llenas, y, si se descuidaban, en los hocicos.

A todo esto, el señor mi amo estaba en el púlpito de rodillas, las manos y los ojos puestos en el cielo, transportado en la divina esencia, que el planto y ruido y voces que en la iglesia había no eran parte para apartalle de su divina contemplación.

Aquellos buenos hombres llegaron a él, y dando voces le despertaron, y le suplicaron quisiese socorrer a aquel pobre, que estaba muriendo, y que no mirase a las cosas pasadas ni a sus dichos malos, pues ya dellos tenía el pago; mas si en algo podría aprovechar para librarle del peligro y pasión que padecía, por amor de Dios lo hiciese, pues ellos veían clara la culpa del

impossible, but everything is possible, You know the truth and how unjustly I have been insulted. As far as I am concerned, I forgive him, so that You, Lord, may forgive me. Pay no mind to the man who knows not what he does or says. But, as for the insult given to You, I beseech You, and ask You out of justice, don't overlook it; because some of those present, who might have planned to buy this holy indulgence, may lend credence to that man's false words, and might decide not to do so. Since it is such a detriment to my fellow man, I beseech You, Lord, don't overlook it, but perform some miracle here at once, and of this nature: If what he says is true, and I am false and evil, let this pulpit sink with me fifty feet into the earth, and let it and me never be seen again. But if what I say is true, and that man, won over by the Devil (in order to rob and deprive those present of such a great benefit), speaks wickedness, let *him* be punished so that all men know his evil ways."

My pious master had scarcely ended his prayer, when that damned constable fainted away, hitting the floor with such a loud thud that the whole church re-echoed. Then he started to bellow, foam at the mouth, twist his mouth, make terrible faces, strike out with his hands and feet, and roll around the floor from side to side.

The racket and the people's shouting were so loud that they couldn't hear one another. A few were alarmed and afraid. Some said: "May the Lord aid and assist him!" Others: "He deserves it, because he was bearing such false witness."

Finally a few of those present, not without great fear, it seemed to me, went up to him and seized his arms, with which he was delivering hard punches to those within reach. Others pulled him by the legs and held him fast, because there wasn't a vicious mule in the world that gave such hard kicks. And they held him that way for some time; more than fifteen men were all over him, and he gave them all a hard time, and, if they were careless, a punch in the nose.

While all this was happening, my lord and master was kneeling in the pulpit, his hands clasped and his eyes fixed on heaven, transported into the divine essence; the weeping, noise, and shouts in the church had no power to pry him out of his holy meditation.

Those good men went up to him, and woke him up with their shouts; they begged him to be good enough to aid that poor man who was dying. Let him pay no mind to what had occurred or to his opponent's spiteful words, since he was already paying for them; if he could do anything to free him from the dangerous state he was in, let him do so for the love of God, because they clearly saw the guilty man's guilt, and

culpado, y la verdad y bondad suya, pues a su petición y venganza el Señor no alargó el castigo.

El señor comisario, como quien despierta de un dulce sueño, los miró, y miró al delincuente y a todos los que alderredor estaban, y muy pausadamente les dijo: —Buenos hombres, vosotros nunca habíades de rogar por un hombre en quien Dios tan señaladamente se ha señalado; mas, pues Él nos manda que no volvamos mal por mal, y perdonemos las injurias, con confianza podremos suplicarle que cumpla lo que nos manda y Su Majestad perdone a éste, que le ofendió poniendo en su santa fe obstáculo. Vamos todos a suplicalle.

Y así, bajó del púlpito y encomendó a que muy devotamente suplicasen a Nuestro Señor tuviese por bien de perdonar a aquel pecador y volverle en su salud y sano juicio, y lanzar dél el demonio, si Su Majestad había permitido que por su gran pecado en él entrase.

Todos se hincaron de rodillas, y delante del altar, con los clérigos, comenzaban a cantar con voz baja una letanía. Y viviendo él con la cruz y agua bendita, después de haber sobre él cantado, el señor mi amo, puestas las manos al cielo y los ojos que casi nada se le parecía sino un poco de blanco, comienza una oración no menos larga que devota, con la cual hizo llorar a toda la gente (como suelen hacer en los sermones de Pasión, de predicador y auditorio devoto), suplicando a Nuestro Señor, pues no quería la muerte del pecador, sino su vida y arrepentimiento, que aquel encaminado por el demonio y persuadido de la muerte y pecado, le quisiese perdonar y dar vida y salud, para que se arrepintiese y confesase sus pecados.

Y esto hecho, mandó traer la bula y púsosela en la cabeza. Y luego el pecador del alguacil comenzó, poco a poco, a estar mejor y tornar en sí. Y desque fue bien vuelto en su acuerdo, echóse a los pies del señor comisario y demandóle perdón; y confesó haber dicho aquello por la boca y mandamiento del demonio, lo uno, por hacer a él daño y vengarse del enojo; lo otro, y más principal, porque el demonio reciba mucha pena del bien que allí se hiciera en tomar la bula.

El señor mi amo le perdonó, y fueron hechas las amistades entre ellos. Y a tomar la bula hubo tanta priesa, que casi ánima viviente en el lugar no quedó sin ella, marido y mujer, y hijos y hijas, mozos y mozas.

Divulgóse la nueva de lo acaecido por los lugares comarcanos,

the preacher's truthfulness and goodness, since when he called for retribution, the Lord didn't defer the punishment for one minute.

The commissioner, like a man awakening from a gentle slumber, looked at them, looked at the offender and at all those standing around, and said very calmly: "Good people, there was no cause for you to pray for a man in whom God has so manifestly shown His anger; but, since He commands us not to return evil for evil, but to forgive insults to us, we can confidently beseech Him to observe His own commandment to us; may His Majesty forgive this man, who offended Him by setting impediments to His holy religion. Let us all beseech Him."

And so, he descended from the pulpit and urged everyone to pray very devoutly to Our Lord to deign to pardon that sinner and restore his health and reason, casting the Devil out of him, if His Majesty had allowed him to enter his body on account of his great sin.

All present fell to their knees, and, in front of the altar, along with the priests, they started to chant a quiet litany. My lord and master, coming with a cross and holy water, chanted over the victim, clasped his hands together, and raised his eyes to heaven, so that almost nothing could be seen of them except a little of their white; then he began a prayer as lengthy as it was pious, which made everyone weep (as generally occurs at Good Friday sermons, when the preacher and the listeners are devout); in it he begged Our Lord, who does not desire the death of a sinner, but his life in a state of repentance, to deign to pardon and give life and health to that man who had been directed by the Devil and led astray on the path of death and sin; thus, he would repent and confess his sins.

After that, he asked for a copy of the indulgence and placed it on the victim's head. Immediately that sinful constable began to get better gradually and come to his senses. After his reason was fully restored, he threw himself at the commissioner's feet and asked for his forgiveness. He confessed that he had said what he did at the Devil's dictation and command, for two reasons: first, to do the commissioner harm and avenge himself for his vexation; second (the chief reason), because the Devil derives great pain from the benefit the people there would gain by buying the indulgence.

My master forgave him, and they renewed their friendship. Then there was such eagerness to buy the indulgence that there was hardly a living soul in the village who didn't acquire one, husbands and wives, sons and daughters, man- and maidservants.

The news of the event spread through the nearby villages, and

y, cuando a ellos llegábamos, no era menester sermón ni ir a la iglesia, que a la posada la venían a tomar, como si fueran peras que se dieran de balde. De manera que, en diez o doce lugares de aquellos alderredores donde fuimos, echó el señor mi amo otras tantas mil bulas sin predicar sermón.

Cuando él hizo el ensayo, confieso mi pecado que también fui dello espantado, y creí que ansí era, como otros muchos; mas con ver después la risa y burla que mi amo y el alguacil llevaban y hacían del negocio, conocí cómo había sido industriado por el industrioso y inventivo de mi amo.

[Acaeciónos en otro lugar, el cual no quiero nombrar por su honra, lo siguiente, y fue que mi amo predicó dos o tres sermones, y dó a Dios la bula tomaban. Visto por el astuto de mi amo lo que pasaba, y que aunque decía se fiaban por un año no aprovechaba, y que estaban tan rebeldes en tomarla, y que su trabajo era perdido, hizo tocar las campanas para despedirse, y hecho su sermón y despedido desde el púlpito, ya que se quería abajar, llamó al escribano y a mí, que iba cargado con unas alforjas, y hízonos llegar al primer escalón, y tomó al alguacil las que en las manos llevaba, y las que yo tenía en las alforjas púsolas junto a sus pies, y tornóse a poner en el púlpito con cara alegre, y arrojar desde allí, de diez en diez y de veinte en veinte, de sus bulas hacia todas partes, diciendo:

—Hermanos míos, tomad, tomad de las gracias que Dios os envía hasta vuestras casas, y no os duela, pues es obra tan pía la redención de los cautivos cristianos que están en tierra de moros, porque no renieguen nuestra santa fe y vayan a las penas del infierno, siquiera ayudaldes con vuestra limosna, y con cinco Pater nostres y cinco Ave marías, para que salgan de cautiverio. Y aun también aprovechan para los padres y hermanos y deudos que tenéis en el Purgatorio, como lo veréis en esta santa bula.

Como el pueblo las vio ansí arrojar, como cosa que la daba de balde y ser venida de la mano de Dios, tomaban a más tomar, aun para los niños de la cuna y para todos sus defuntos contando desde los hijos hasta el menor criado que tenían, contándolos por los dedos. Vímonos en tanta priesa, que a mí aínas me acabaron de romper un pobre y viejo sayo que traía; de manera

when we got to them, there was no need of a sermon or a church service, because people came to our inn to buy, as if the indulgences
were pears given away free. So that, in ten or twelve villages we vis-
ited in that vicinity, my master unloaded ten or twelve thousand indulgences without preaching a sermon.

When he played that trick, I confess, to my discredit, that I was
frightened by it, too, thinking, like many other people, that it really happened that way. But later, when I observed the way my master and the
constable were laughing and showing their contempt over that deal, I
realized that it had been a scheme of my scheming, inventive master.[72]

[We had the following experience in another village, whose name I
won't mention to safeguard its honor. My master preached two or
three sermons, but not a solitary indulgence was bought. When my
clever master saw the way things were going, and that he was getting
nowhere even when he offered the indulgences on credit for a year,
but the people were so set against buying them, and his labors were
in vain, he ordered the church bells rung for a concluding sermon.
After giving it and closing the ceremony from the pulpit, when he was
about to descend, he called the clerk and me (I was loaded down with
several saddlebags) and summoned us over to the first step. He took
from the constable the copies of the indulgence that he had in his
hands, and he placed those I had in the saddlebags next to his feet. He
returned to the pulpit with a cheerful face, and from there he flung
his indulgences by tens and twenties in every direction, saying:

"Brothers, take them, receive of the grace that God is sending to
your homes, and have no regrets, because it is such a pious work to
ransom Christian captives in Moorish lands, so that they do not re-
nounce our holy religion and thus suffer in Hell. Just aid them with
your alms, and with five Our Fathers and five Hail Marys, so that they
are released from captivity. And these indulgences are also good for
your parents, brothers and sisters, and other relatives in Purgatory, as
you will see when you read this holy certificate."

When the people saw him flinging them out that way, like a thing
given away free and handed out without working for it, they took all
they could, even for the babies in the cradle, and for all their deceased
family members, from their children down to their humblest servant,
counting them on their fingers. We found ourselves in such a crush
that they nearly managed to rip a wretched old shirt I was wearing. So

---

72. The following long passage enclosed in square brackets is an interpolation
found in the Alcalá edition of 1554.

que certifico a Vuestra Merced que en poco más de una hora no quedó bula en las alforjas, y fue necesario ir a la posada por más.

Acabados de tomar todos, dijo mi amo desde el púlpito a su escribano y al del Consejo que se levantasen, y para que se supiese quién eran los que habían de gozar de la santa indulgencia y perdones de la santa bula y para que él diese buena cuenta a quien le había enviado, se escribiesen.

Y así, luego todos de muy buena voluntad decían las que habían tomado, contando por orden los hijos y criados y defuntos.

Hecho su inventario, pidió a los alcaldes que, por caridad, porque él tenía que hacer en otra parte, mandasen al escribano le diese autoridad del inventario y memoria de las que allí quedaban, que, según decía el escribano, eran más de dos mil.

Hecho esto, él se despidió con mucha paz y amor, y ansí nos partimos deste lugar. Y aun antes que nos partiésemos, fue preguntado él por el teniente cura del lugar y por los regidores si la bula aprovechaba para las criaturas que estaban en el vientre de sus madres. A lo cual él respondió que, según las letras que él había estudiado, que no, que lo fuesen a preguntar a los doctores más antiguos que él, y que esto era lo que sentía en este negocio.

E ansí nos partimos, yendo todos muy alegres del buen negocio. Decía mi amo al alguacil y escribano: —¿Qué os parece, cómo a estos villanos, que con sólo decir cristianos viejos somos, sin hacer obras de caridad se piensan salvar, sin poner nada de su hacienda? Pues, ¡por vida del licenciado Pascasio Gómez, que a su costa se saquen más de diez cautivos!

Y ansí nos fuimos hasta otro lugar de aquel cabo de Toledo, hacia la Mancha, que se dice, adonde topamos otros más obstinados en tomar bulas. Hechas mi amo y los demás que íbamos nuestras diligencias, en dos fiestas que allí estuvimos no se habían echado treinta bulas.

Visto por mi amo la gran perdición y la mucha costa que traía, y el ardideza que el sotil de mi amo tuvo para hacer desprender sus bulas fue que este día dijo la misa mayor, y después de

that I guarantee Your Honor that, in a little over an hour, there wasn't an indulgence left in the saddlebags, and we had to go back to the inn for more.

When everyone had taken some, my master, still in the pulpit, asked his clerk and the clerk of the town council to get up and take down the names of the recipients, so that it might be known who was to enjoy the benefits of the holy indulgence and the pardons granted by the papal bull, and so that he could make a strict accounting to those who had sent him.

And so, everyone immediately reported very gladly how many they had taken, counting up their children, servants, and departed kin in orderly fashion.

When his roster was completed, he asked the village magistrates— he himself, he said, had urgent business elsewhere—to be kind enough to order the clerk to send him a notarized copy of the roster and a record of the indulgences left there, which, according to the clerk, came to over two thousand.[73]

Thereupon he took his leave in an atmosphere of peace and love, and so we departed from that village. But even before we left, he was asked by the assistant to the parish priest of the village and by the magistrates whether the indulgence covered infants still in their mother's womb. He said that, in the light of the books he had studied, he didn't think so; they should go ask theologians who were older than himself; that was his only regret in these dealings.

And so we left, all happy over the good business deal. My master said to his constable and clerk: "What do you think about these rustics, who think they can be saved merely by saying 'we're Old Christians,'[74] and without doing works of charity or spending any of their money? Well, by the life of the graduate Pascasio Gómez, let more than ten captives be ransomed at their expense!"

And so we headed for another village on the outskirts of Toledo, on the way to La Mancha, as it's called, where we ran across others even more dead set against buying indulgences. After my master and we others with him had taken our preliminary measures, on the two feast days during our stay there we hadn't unloaded thirty indulgences.

When my master saw how much he was losing and how much he was spending, he cleverly conceived the following ploy for getting rid of his indulgences. That day, he said High Mass. When he had finished

---

73. Apparently, with these documents in hand, the money could be collected later on, though the villagers seem unaware of this, despite the offer of credit.   74. That is, not converts from Islam or Judaism.

acabado el sermón y vuelto al altar, tomó una cruz que traía de poco más de un palmo, y en un brasero de lumbre que encima del altar había (el cual habían traído para calentarse las manos, porque hacía gran frío), púsole detrás del misal, sin que nadie mirase en ello. Y allí, sin decir nada, puso la cruz encima la lumbre, y ya que hubo acabado la misa y echada la bendición, tomóla con un pañizuelo bien envuelta la cruz en la mano derecha y en la otra la bula, y ansí se bajó hasta la postrera grada del altar, adonde hizo que besaba la cruz. Y hizo señal que viniesen adorar la cruz. Y ansí vinieron los alcaldes los primeros y los más ancianos del lugar, viniendo uno a uno, como se usa.

Y el primero que llegó, que era un alcalde viejo, aunque él le dio a besar la cruz bien delicadamente, se abrasó los rostros y se quitó presto a fuera. Lo cual visto por mi amo, le dijo: —¡Paso quedo, señor alcalde! ¡Milagro!

Y ansí hicieron otros siete o ocho. Y a todos les decía: —¡Paso, señores! ¡Milagro!

Cuando él vido que los rostriquemados bastaban para testigos del milagro, no la quiso dar más a besar. Subióse al pie del altar y de allí decía cosas maravillosas, diciendo que por la poca caridad que había en ellos había Dios permitido aquel milagro, y que aquella cruz había de ser llevada a la santa iglesia mayor de su obispado, que por la poca caridad que en el pueblo había, la cruz ardía.

Fue tanta la prisa que hubo en el tomar de la bula, que no bastaban dos escribanos ni los clérigos ni sacristanes a escribir. Creo de cierto que se tomaron más de tres mil bulas, como tengo dicho a Vuestra Merced.

Después, al partir, él fue con gran reverencia, como es razón, a tomar la santa cruz, diciendo que la había de hacer engastonar en oro, como era razón. Fue rogado mucho del Concejo y clérigos del lugar les dejase allí aquella santa cruz, por memoria del milagro allí acaecido. Él en ninguna manera lo quería hacer, y al fin, rogado de tantos, se la dejó; con que le dieron otra cruz vieja que tenían, antigua, de plata, que podrá pesar dos o tres libras, según decían.

Y ansí nos partimos alegres con el buen trueque y con haber negociado bien. En todo no vio nadie lo suso dicho sino yo. Porque me subí a par del altar para ver si había quedado algo en las ampollas, para ponello en cobro, como otras veces yo lo tenía de costumbre, y como allí me vio, púsose el dedo en la boca,

his sermon and returned to the altar, he took a cross he had, not much bigger than a span, and, without anyone noticing it, placed it behind the missal in a brazier that stood on top of the altar (they had brought it for him to warm his hands, because it was a very cold day). There, without saying a word, he put the cross on the fire and, when he had finished the Mass and pronounced the benediction, he picked up the cross, thickly wrapped in a piece of cloth, with his right hand and a copy of the indulgence with his left, and walked down to the lowest step of the altar, where he pretended to kiss the cross. He made a sign for people to come and worship the cross. And so the magistrates and the village elders came first, going up one at a time as customary.

The first man who came, an aged magistrate, burned his mouth, even though my master gave him the cross to kiss very gently, and he left the spot quickly. When my master saw this, he said to him: "Take careful note, magistrate! A miracle!"

The same thing occurred with seven or eight others. To each one he said: "Take note, gentlemen! A miracle!"

When he saw that those with burnt faces were sufficient as witnesses to the miracle, he didn't give the cross to anyone else to kiss. He ascended to the foot of the altar and from there he said wonderful things, declaring that God had permitted that miracle because of the lack of charity they displayed; that cross would have to be brought to the holy cathedral in his bishopric, because, to show that village's lack of charity, it had started to burn.

There was such a crush of people to buy indulgences that the two clerks, the priests, and the sacristans couldn't record all their names. I firmly believe that over three thousand were bought, as I've told Your Honor.

Later, when we were leaving, he went, with all the great reverence due, to take that holy cross, saying that he must have it mounted in gold, which was only right. He was ardently begged by the village council and the local priests to leave them that holy cross in memory of the miracle that had occurred there. He refused absolutely, but finally, when so many people were pleading for it, he left it there. In exchange they gave him another old cross they owned, an antique made of silver and probably weighing two or three pounds, according to their statement.

And so we departed merrily because of that profitable exchange and the good business we had done. No one but myself saw the actions I have described. Because I had gone up close to the altar to see if any Communion wine was left in the flasks, so I could store it away as I usually did; and when he saw me there, he put his finger to his

haciéndome señal que callase. Yo ansí lo hice, porque me cumplía, aunque después que vi el milagro no cabía en mí por echallo fuera, sino que el temor de mi astuto amo no me lo dejaba comunicar con nadie, ni nunca de mí salió. Porque me tomó juramento que no descubriese el milagro, y ansí lo hice hasta agora.]

Y aunque mochacho, cayóme mucho en gracia y dije entre mí: "¡Cuántas déstas deben hacer estos burladores entre la inocente gente!"

Finalmente, estuve con este mi quinto amo cerca de cuatro meses, en los cuales pasé también hartas fatigas, [aunque me daba bien de comer, a costa de los curas y otros clérigos do iba a predicar].

## TRATADO SEXTO

### Cómo Lázaro se asentó con un capellán y lo que con él pasó

Después desto, asenté con un maestro de pintar panderos para molelle los colores, y también sufrí mil males.

Siendo ya en este tiempo buen mozuelo, entrando un día en la iglesia mayor, un capellán della me recibió por suyo. Y púsome en poder un asno y cuatro cántaros, y un azote, y comencé a echar agua por la ciudad. Este fue el primer escalón que yo subí para venir a alcanzar buena vida, porque mi boca era medida. Daba cada día a mi amo treinta maravedís ganados, y los sábados ganaba para mí, y todo lo demás, entre semana, de treinta maravedís.

Fueme tan bien en el oficio, que al cabo de cuatro años que lo usé, con poner en la ganancia buen recaudo, ahorré para me vestir muy honradamente de la ropa vieja. De la cual compré un jubón de fustán viejo y un sayo raído, de manga tranzada y puerta, y una capa que había sido frisada, y una espada de las viejas primeras de Cuéllar. Desque me vi en hábito de hombre de bien, dije a mi amo se tomase su asno, que no quería más seguir aquel oficio.

lips as a sign that I should keep quiet. And so I did, because it was my duty; though, after seeing the miracle, I was unable to reveal the truth—fear of my sly master kept me from telling anyone about it, and I never did. Because he made me swear never to explain the miracle, and I've kept quiet to this very day.]

Though I was just a boy, I found this very funny, and I said to myself: "How many such tricks these sharpsters must play on innocent people!"

The long and the short of it was that I remained with this fifth master of mine for about four months, in the course of which I also underwent plenty of labors,[75] [although he gave me enough to eat, at the expense of the curates and other priests in the places where he went to preach].

## CHAPTER SIX

### How Lázaro Was Employed by a Chaplain, and What Befell Him in His Company

After that I took a job with a painter of tambourines,[76] to grind his colors. There, too, I suffered a thousand griefs.

Being a sturdy, older boy by this time, one day when I went into the cathedral, I was hired by one of the chaplains.[77] He placed in my keeping a donkey, four large pitchers, and a whip, and I started to sell water on the streets of the city. This was the first rung on the ladder I have climbed to reach a good life, because my voice was suited to the calling. Every weekday I handed over to my master thirty *maravedís* that I had taken in; on Saturdays all the income was for me, as was anything over the daily thirty *maravedís* during the week.

I did so well at that job that, after working at it for four years and taking good care of my earnings, I had saved up enough to outfit myself quite respectably at an old-clothes dealer's. I bought an old fustian doublet and a worn-out tunic with braided sleeves and trimming in front, a cloak that had once had a curled nap, and a sword that was one of the first made in Cuéllar[78] way back when. Once I saw myself dressed like a worthy citizen, I told my master to take back his donkey, because I didn't want to do that kind of work anymore.

75. The following bracketed words are an interpolation in the Alcalá edition.   76. These painters generally peddled their tambourines.   77. Priests in charge of the individual chapels in the cathedral.   78. A town near Segovia famous for its swords many decades before the time of the story.

## TRATADO SÉPTIMO

### Cómo Lázaro se asentó con un alguacil
### y de lo que le acaeció con él

Despedido del capellán, asenté por hombre de justicia con un
alguacil. Mas muy poco viví con él, por parecerme oficio peli-
groso. Mayormente, que una noche nos corrieron a mí y a mi
amo a pedradas y a palos unos retraídos. Y a mi amo, que esperó,
trataron mal, mas a mí no me alcanzaron. Con esto renegué del
trato.

Y pensando en qué modo de vivir haría mi asiento, por tener
descanso y ganar algo para la vejez, quiso Dios alumbrarme, y
ponerme en camino y manera provechosa. Y con favor que tuve
de amigos y señores, todos mis trabajos y fatigas hasta entonces
pasados fueron pagados con alcanzar lo que procuré: que fue un
oficio real, viendo que no hay nadie que medre, sino los que le
tienen.

En el cual el día de hoy vivo y resido a servicio de Dios y de
Vuestra Merced. Y es que tengo cargo de pregonar los vinos que
en esta ciudad se venden, y en almonedas y cosas perdidas;
acompañar los que padecen persecuciones por justicia y declarar
a voces sus delitos: pregonero, hablando en buen romance.

[En el cual oficio, un día que ahorcábamos un apañador en
Toledo, y llevaba una buena soga de esparto, conocí y caí en la
cuenta de la sentencia que aquel mi ciego amo había dicho en
Escalona, y me arrepentí del mal pago que le di, por lo mucho
que me enseñó. Que, después de Dios, él me dio industria para
llegar al estado que ahora estó.]

Hame sucedido tan bien, yo le he usado tan fácilmente, que
casi todas las cosas al oficio tocantes pasan por mi mano. Tanto,
que, en toda la ciudad, el que ha de echar vino a vender, o algo,
si Lázaro de Tormes no entiende en ello, hacen cuenta de no
sacar provecho.

En este tiempo, viendo mi habilidad y buen vivir, teniendo
noticia de mi persona el señor arcipreste de San Salvador, mi

## CHAPTER SEVEN

## How Lázaro Was Employed by a Constable, and What Happened to Him in His Company

After taking leave of the chaplain, I hired myself out to a constable as an assistant lawman. But I remained with him only briefly, because I found it a dangerous job. One night, especially, some criminals[79] chased my master and me, brandishing clubs and throwing stones. My master stood his ground and was badly hurt, but they didn't catch me. After that, I reneged on the deal.

While I was pondering over what kind of work to take up permanently, so I could enjoy some peace and save up something for my old age, God was pleased to enlighten me and guide my steps in a profitable direction. With the aid of friends and influential people, all the labors and griefs I had undergone up till then were compensated when I obtained the position I sought—a government employment—because no one prospers who doesn't have one of those.

And I still have it today, residing here at the service of God and Your Honor's. My job is to cry the wines that are sold in this city,[80] to act as auctioneer, and to announce that items have been lost; and also to accompany those who are judicially punished, calling out their crimes—to put it in plain language, I'm a town crier.[81]

[On this job, one day when we were hanging a thief in Toledo, and I was carrying a strong rope of esparto grass, I remembered the prophecy that my blind master had uttered in Escalona, and I felt sorry for the bad return I had made him for all that he taught me. Because, after God, it was he who gave me the know-how to get to the position I now occupy.]

I've done so well at this job, which has come to me so naturally, that almost all matters pertaining to the position pass through my hands. So much so, that throughout the city anyone with wine to sell, or other things, imagines he isn't getting his money's worth unless Lázaro de Tormes has a hand in it.

Around this time, seeing my skill and respectable habits, and inquiring more closely about me, the archpriest[82] of San Salvador,[83] my

---

79. Specifically, those who took refuge in churches but sallied out at night to commit crimes.    80. The owners of the wine paid the crier to make a public proclamation that wine was for sale.    81. The following bracketed paragraph is an interpolation in the Alcalá edition.    82. Usually, vicar to a bishop, dean of the cathedral.    83. A parish in Toledo.

señor, y servidor y amigo de Vuestra Merced, porque le prego-
naba sus vinos, procuró casarme con una criada suya. Y visto
por mí que de tal persona no podía venir sino bien y favor,
acordé de lo hacer. Y así, me casé con ella, y hasta agora no
estoy arrepentido.

Porque, allende de ser buena hija y diligente servicial, tengo
en mi señor arcipreste todo favor y ayuda, y siempre en el año le
da en veces al pie de una carga de trigo; por las Pascuas, su
carne; y cuando el par de los bodigos, las calzas viejas que deja.
Y hízonos alquilar una casilla par de la suya. Los domingos y
fiestas casi todas las comíamos en su casa.

Mas malas lenguas, que nunca faltaron ni faltarán, no nos
dejan vivir, diciendo no sé qué y sí sé qué de que veen a mi
mujer irle a hacer la cama y guisalle de comer. Y mejor les ayude
Dios que ellos dicen la verdad.

[Aunque en este tiempo siempre he tenido alguna sos-
pechuela, y habido algunas malas cenas por esperalla algunas
noches hasta las laudes, y aún más; y se me ha venido a la
memoria lo que mi amo el ciego me dijo en Escalona, estando
asido al cuerno. Aunque, de verdad, siempre pienso que el diablo me lo trae a la memoria por hacerme malcasado, y no le
aprovecha.]

Porque, allende de no ser ella mujer que se pague destas
burlas, mi señor me ha prometido lo que pienso cumplirá. Que
él me habló un día muy largo delante della y me dijo:

—Lázaro de Tormes, quien ha de mirar a dichos de malas
lenguas nunca medrará. Digo esto porque no me maravillaría
alguno, viendo entrar en mi casa a tu mujer y salir della. Ella
entra muy a tu honra y suya, y esto te lo prometo. Por tanto, no
mires a lo que puedan decir, sino a lo que te toca, digo, a tu
provecho.

—Señor —le dije—, yo determiné de arrimarme a los
buenos. Verdad es que algunos de mis amigos me han dicho
algo deso, y aun por más de tres veces me han certificado
que antes que comigo casase había parido tres veces,
hablando con reverencia de Vuestra Merced, porque está
ella delante.

master and Your Honor's humble servant and friend, whose wines I
was crying, offered to arrange a marriage for me with one of his servant women. Realizing that such a match could only lead to prosper-
ity and favor, I agreed to enter it. And so, I married her, and I've never
been sorry I did.

Because, besides the fact that she's a good girl and a diligent servant, I enjoy a great deal of favor and assistance from my patron, the
archpriest: at different times in the course of the year he always gives
us something like two hundred liters of wheat; meat at Eastertime;
and, when he gives us a couple of loaves from the offering, I get a pair
of his old breeches as well. He also had us rent a little house near his
own. Almost every Sunday and holiday, we eat in his house.

But slandermongers, of whom there are plenty and always will be,
don't let us live; they say I-don't-know-what and I-do-know-what
when they see my wife go to make his bed and cook his meals. May
God help them if they're telling the truth![84]

[And yet, around that time, I always had some minor doubts; at
times I had miserable suppertimes, waiting as long as Lauds,[85] and
even later, for her to get home, some nights. Then I would remember
what my master, the blind man, told me in Escalona when he was
holding onto the horn. But, to tell the truth, I always believe that the
Devil is making me remember it in order to make me unhappy in my
marriage—though it does him no good.]

Because, besides the fact that she's not the sort of woman to indulge in
such deceptions, my patron has made me a promise that I think he'll keep.
Because one day he made me a long speech in her presence and told me:

"Lázaro de Tormes, no one who pays attention to the sayings of slandermongers will ever prosper. I say this because no such saying would
surprise me, since people see your wife entering and leaving my house.
It is to your complete honor and hers that she does so, I promise you
that. Therefore pay no attention to anything they may say, but give
heed to things that concern you—I mean, that turn to your advantage."

"Sir," I said, "I'm determined to throw in my lot with good people.
It's true that some of my friends have mentioned these rumors to me,
and more than three times they've declared that she gave birth to
three children before marrying me; I apologize to Your Honor for my
crude language, because she's present."[86]

---

84. The implication is that they aren't. The following bracketed paragraph is an interpolation in the Alcalá edition.    85. Ecclesiastical hours usually read right after
Matins, at daybreak.    86. This cumbersome sentence has been interpreted in various
other ways.

Entonces mi mujer echó juramentos sobre sí, que yo pensé la
casa se hundiera con nosotros. Y después tomóse a llorar y a
echar maldiciones sobre quien comigo la había casado. En tal
manera, que quisiera ser muerto antes que se me hubiera
soltado aquella palabra de la boca. Mas yo de un cabo y mi señor
de otro, tanto le dijimos y otorgamos, que cesó su llanto, con juramento que le hice de nunca más en mi vida mentalle nada de
aquello, y que yo holgaba y había por bien de que ella entrase y
saliese, de noche y de día, pues estaba bien seguro de su bondad. Y así quedamos todos tres bien conformes.

Hasta el día de hoy nunca nadie nos oyó sobre el caso; antes,
cuando alguno siento que quiere decir algo della, le atajo y le
digo:

—Mirá, si sois amigo, no me digáis cosa con que me pese, que
no tengo por mi amigo al que me hace pesar; mayormente, si me
quiere meter mal con mi mujer, que es la cosa del mundo que
yo más quiero y la amo más que a mí; y me hace Dios con ella
mil mercedes y más bien que yo merezco; que yo juraré sobre la
hostia consagrada, que es tan buena mujer como vive dentro de
las puertas de Toledo. Quien otra cosa me dijere, yo me mataré
con él. —Desta manera no me dicen nada y yo tengo paz en mi
casa.

Esto fue el mesmo año que nuestro victorioso Emperador en
esta insigne ciudad de Toledo entró, y tuvo en ella Cortes, y se
hicieron grandes regocijos, como Vuestra Merced habrá oído.
Pues en este tiempo estaba en mi prosperidad y en la cumbre de
toda buena fortuna.

[De lo que de aquí adelante me sucediere, avisaré a Vuestra
Merced.]

Then my wife swore so many oaths protesting her innocence that I thought the house would sink into the earth along with us. Then she began to cry and to curse the people who had married her to me. She went on so, that I wished I had died before uttering those words. But we told her and promised her so much, I on one side and my patron on the other, that she stopped crying, after I swore never to mention anything of the sort to her as long as I lived, and assured her that I was pleased, and found it right, that she should go in and out, day or night, because I trusted completely in her chastity. And so all three of us were in agreement.

Up till this day, no one has heard us discuss the matter; in fact, whenever I think that someone is about to mention it, I cut him short with these words:

"See here, if you're my friend, don't tell me anything that will give me pain, because I don't consider anyone who grieves me to be a friend; especially if he wants to put me on bad terms with my wife, because she's the thing I love best in the world—I love her better than I do myself. In her, God shows me a thousand favors, much more than I deserve; for I'll swear on the consecrated Host that she's as good a woman as any dwelling within the gates of Toledo. I'll fight anyone who tells me something different." That way, they tell me nothing, and I enjoy domestic peace.

That was the same year[87] in which our victorious emperor[88] celebrated a formal entrée in this famous city of Toledo, and held a parliament in it; there were great festivities, as Your Honor must have heard. Well, at that time I was prospering and at the pinnacle of my good fortune.

[I'll let Your Honor know about whatever happens to me from now on.][89]

---

87. The dating of the story depends partially on the identification of this date; see the Introduction.   88. Holy Roman Emperor Charles V (King Charles I of Spain). 89. This final interpolation in the Alcalá edition leaves the door wide open to sequels and continuations (which was probably not the original author's intention; see the section "The Continuations" in the Introduction).

A CATALOG OF SELECTED
# DOVER BOOKS
IN ALL FIELDS OF INTEREST

# A CATALOG OF SELECTED DOVER
# BOOKS IN ALL FIELDS OF INTEREST

CONCERNING THE SPIRITUAL IN ART, Wassily Kandinsky. Pioneering work by father of abstract art. Thoughts on color theory, nature of art. Analysis of earlier masters. 12 illustrations. 80pp. of text. 5⅜ x 8½.                           23411-8

ANIMALS: 1,419 Copyright-Free Illustrations of Mammals, Birds, Fish, Insects, etc., Jim Harter (ed.). Clear wood engravings present, in extremely lifelike poses, over 1,000 species of animals. One of the most extensive pictorial sourcebooks of its kind. Captions. Index. 284pp. 9 x 12.                           23766-4

CELTIC ART: The Methods of Construction, George Bain. Simple geometric techniques for making Celtic interlacements, spirals, Kells-type initials, animals, humans, etc. Over 500 illustrations. 160pp. 9 x 12. (Available in U.S. only.)                           22923-8

AN ATLAS OF ANATOMY FOR ARTISTS, Fritz Schider. Most thorough reference work on art anatomy in the world. Hundreds of illustrations, including selections from works by Vesalius, Leonardo, Goya, Ingres, Michelangelo, others. 593 illustrations. 192pp. 7⅛ x 10¼.                           20241-0

CELTIC HAND STROKE-BY-STROKE (Irish Half-Uncial from "The Book of Kells"): An Arthur Baker Calligraphy Manual, Arthur Baker. Complete guide to creating each letter of the alphabet in distinctive Celtic manner. Covers hand position, strokes, pens, inks, paper, more. Illustrated. 48pp. 8¼ x 11.                           24336-2

EASY ORIGAMI, John Montroll. Charming collection of 32 projects (hat, cup, pelican, piano, swan, many more) specially designed for the novice origami hobbyist. Clearly illustrated easy-to-follow instructions insure that even beginning papercrafters will achieve successful results. 48pp. 8¼ x 11.                           27298 2

THE COMPLETE BOOK OF BIRDHOUSE CONSTRUCTION FOR WOODWORKERS, Scott D. Campbell. Detailed instructions, illustrations, tables. Also data on bird habitat and instinct patterns. Bibliography. 3 tables. 63 illustrations in 15 figures. 48pp. 5¼ x 8½.                           24407-5

BLOOMINGDALE'S ILLUSTRATED 1886 CATALOG: Fashions, Dry Goods and Housewares, Bloomingdale Brothers. Famed merchants' extremely rare catalog depicting about 1,700 products: clothing, housewares, firearms, dry goods, jewelry, more. Invaluable for dating, identifying vintage items. Also, copyright-free graphics for artists, designers. Co-published with Henry Ford Museum & Greenfield Village. 160pp. 8¼ x 11.                           25780-0

HISTORIC COSTUME IN PICTURES, Braun & Schneider. Over 1,450 costumed figures in clearly detailed engravings–from dawn of civilization to end of 19th century. Captions. Many folk costumes. 256pp. 8⅜ x 11¾.                           23150-X

STICKLEY CRAFTSMAN FURNITURE CATALOGS, Gustav Stickley and L. & J. G. Stickley. Beautiful, functional furniture in two authentic catalogs from 1910. 594 illustrations, including 277 photos, show settles, rockers, armchairs, reclining chairs, bookcases, desks, tables. 183pp. 6½ x 9¼. 23838-5

AMERICAN LOCOMOTIVES IN HISTORIC PHOTOGRAPHS: 1858 to 1949, Ron Ziel (ed.). A rare collection of 126 meticulously detailed official photographs, called "builder portraits," of American locomotives that majestically chronicle the rise of steam locomotive power in America. Introduction. Detailed captions. xi+ 129pp. 9 x 12. 27393-8

AMERICA'S LIGHTHOUSES: An Illustrated History, Francis Ross Holland, Jr. Delightfully written, profusely illustrated fact-filled survey of over 200 American lighthouses since 1716. History, anecdotes, technological advances, more. 240pp. 8 x 10¾. 25576-X

TOWARDS A NEW ARCHITECTURE, Le Corbusier. Pioneering manifesto by founder of "International School." Technical and aesthetic theories, views of industry, economics, relation of form to function, "mass-production split" and much more. Profusely illustrated. 320pp. 6⅛ x 9¼. (Available in U.S. only.) 25023-7

HOW THE OTHER HALF LIVES, Jacob Riis. Famous journalistic record, exposing poverty and degradation of New York slums around 1900, by major social reformer. 100 striking and influential photographs. 233pp. 10 x 7⅞. 22012-5

FRUIT KEY AND TWIG KEY TO TREES AND SHRUBS, William M. Harlow. One of the handiest and most widely used identification aids. Fruit key covers 120 deciduous and evergreen species; twig key 160 deciduous species. Easily used. Over 300 photographs. 126pp. 5⅜ x 8½. 20511-8

COMMON BIRD SONGS, Dr. Donald J. Borror. Songs of 60 most common U.S. birds: robins, sparrows, cardinals, bluejays, finches, more—arranged in order of increasing complexity. Up to 9 variations of songs of each species.
Cassette and manual 99911-4

ORCHIDS AS HOUSE PLANTS, Rebecca Tyson Northen. Grow cattleyas and many other kinds of orchids—in a window, in a case, or under artificial light. 63 illustrations. 148pp. 5⅜ x 8½. 23261-1

MONSTER MAZES, Dave Phillips. Masterful mazes at four levels of difficulty. Avoid deadly perils and evil creatures to find magical treasures. Solutions for all 32 exciting illustrated puzzles. 48pp. 8¼ x 11. 26005-4

MOZART'S DON GIOVANNI (DOVER OPERA LIBRETTO SERIES), Wolfgang Amadeus Mozart. Introduced and translated by Ellen H. Bleiler. Standard Italian libretto, with complete English translation. Convenient and thoroughly portable—an ideal companion for reading along with a recording or the performance itself. Introduction. List of characters. Plot summary. 121pp. 5¼ x 8½. 24944-1

TECHNICAL MANUAL AND DICTIONARY OF CLASSICAL BALLET, Gail Grant. Defines, explains, comments on steps, movements, poses and concepts. 15-page pictorial section. Basic book for student, viewer. 127pp. 5⅜ x 8½. 21843-0

THE CLARINET AND CLARINET PLAYING, David Pino. Lively, comprehensive work features suggestions about technique, musicianship, and musical interpretation, as well as guidelines for teaching, making your own reeds, and preparing for public performance. Includes an intriguing look at clarinet history. "A godsend," *The Clarinet*, Journal of the International Clarinet Society. Appendixes. 7 illus. 320pp. 5⅜ x 8½. 40270-3

HOLLYWOOD GLAMOR PORTRAITS, John Kobal (ed.). 145 photos from 1926-49. Harlow, Gable, Bogart, Bacall; 94 stars in all. Full background on photographers, technical aspects. 160pp. 8⅜ x 11¼. 23352-9

THE ANNOTATED CASEY AT THE BAT: A Collection of Ballads about the Mighty Casey/Third, Revised Edition, Martin Gardner (ed.). Amusing sequels and parodies of one of America's best-loved poems: Casey's Revenge, Why Casey Whiffed, Casey's Sister at the Bat, others. 256pp. 5⅜ x 8½. 28598-7

THE RAVEN AND OTHER FAVORITE POEMS, Edgar Allan Poe. Over 40 of the author's most memorable poems: "The Bells," "Ulalume," "Israfel," "To Helen," "The Conqueror Worm," "Eldorado," "Annabel Lee," many more. Alphabetic lists of titles and first lines. 64pp. 5$\frac{3}{16}$ x 8¼. 26685-0

PERSONAL MEMOIRS OF U. S. GRANT, Ulysses Simpson Grant. Intelligent, deeply moving firsthand account of Civil War campaigns, considered by many the finest military memoirs ever written. Includes letters, historic photographs, maps and more. 528pp. 6⅛ x 9¼. 28587-1

ANCIENT EGYPTIAN MATERIALS AND INDUSTRIES, A. Lucas and J. Harris. Fascinating, comprehensive, thoroughly documented text describes this ancient civilization's vast resources and the processes that incorporated them in daily life, including the use of animal products, building materials, cosmetics, perfumes and incense, fibers, glazed ware, glass and its manufacture, materials used in the mummification process, and much more. 544pp. 6⅛ x 9¼. (Available in U.S. only.) 40446-3

RUSSIAN STORIES/RUSSKIE RASSKAZY: A Dual-Language Book, edited by Gleb Struve. Twelve tales by such masters as Chekhov, Tolstoy, Dostoevsky, Pushkin, others. Excellent word-for-word English translations on facing pages, plus teaching and study aids, Russian/English vocabulary, biographical/critical introductions, more. 416pp. 5⅜ x 8½. 26244-8

PHILADELPHIA THEN AND NOW: 60 Sites Photographed in the Past and Present, Kenneth Finkel and Susan Oyama. Rare photographs of City Hall, Logan Square, Independence Hall, Betsy Ross House, other landmarks juxtaposed with contemporary views. Captures changing face of historic city. Introduction. Captions. 128pp. 8¼ x 11. 25790-8

AIA ARCHITECTURAL GUIDE TO NASSAU AND SUFFOLK COUNTIES, LONG ISLAND, The American Institute of Architects, Long Island Chapter, and the Society for the Preservation of Long Island Antiquities. Comprehensive, well-researched and generously illustrated volume brings to life over three centuries of Long Island's great architectural heritage. More than 240 photographs with authoritative, extensively detailed captions. 176pp. 8¼ x 11. 26946-9

NORTH AMERICAN INDIAN LIFE: Customs and Traditions of 23 Tribes, Elsie Clews Parsons (ed.). 27 fictionalized essays by noted anthropologists examine religion, customs, government, additional facets of life among the Winnebago, Crow, Zuni, Eskimo, other tribes. 480pp. 6⅛ x 9¼. 27377-6

FRANK LLOYD WRIGHT'S DANA HOUSE, Donald Hoffmann. Pictorial essay of residential masterpiece with over 160 interior and exterior photos, plans, elevations, sketches and studies. 128pp. 9¼ x 10¾. 29120-0

THE MALE AND FEMALE FIGURE IN MOTION: 60 Classic Photographic Sequences, Eadweard Muybridge. 60 true-action photographs of men and women walking, running, climbing, bending, turning, etc., reproduced from rare 19th-century masterpiece. vi + 121pp. 9 x 12. 24745-7

1001 QUESTIONS ANSWERED ABOUT THE SEASHORE, N. J. Berrill and Jacquelyn Berrill. Queries answered about dolphins, sea snails, sponges, starfish, fishes, shore birds, many others. Covers appearance, breeding, growth, feeding, much more. 305pp. 5¼ x 8¼. 23366-9

ATTRACTING BIRDS TO YOUR YARD, William J. Weber. Easy-to-follow guide offers advice on how to attract the greatest diversity of birds: birdhouses, feeders, water and waterers, much more. 96pp. 5³⁄₁₆ x 8¼. 28927-3

MEDICINAL AND OTHER USES OF NORTH AMERICAN PLANTS: A Historical Survey with Special Reference to the Eastern Indian Tribes, Charlotte Erichsen-Brown. Chronological historical citations document 500 years of usage of plants, trees, shrubs native to eastern Canada, northeastern U.S. Also complete identifying information. 343 illustrations. 544pp. 6½ x 9¼. 25951-X

STORYBOOK MAZES, Dave Phillips. 23 stories and mazes on two-page spreads: Wizard of Oz, Treasure Island, Robin Hood, etc. Solutions. 64pp. 8¼ x 11. 23628-5

AMERICAN NEGRO SONGS: 230 Folk Songs and Spirituals, Religious and Secular, John W. Work. This authoritative study traces the African influences of songs sung and played by black Americans at work, in church, and as entertainment. The author discusses the lyric significance of such songs as "Swing Low, Sweet Chariot," "John Henry," and others and offers the words and music for 230 songs. Bibliography. Index of Song Titles. 272pp. 6½ x 9¼. 40271-1

MOVIE-STAR PORTRAITS OF THE FORTIES, John Kobal (ed.). 163 glamor, studio photos of 106 stars of the 1940s: Rita Hayworth, Ava Gardner, Marlon Brando, Clark Gable, many more. 176pp. 8⅜ x 11¼. 23546-7

BENCHLEY LOST AND FOUND, Robert Benchley. Finest humor from early 30s, about pet peeves, child psychologists, post office and others. Mostly unavailable elsewhere. 73 illustrations by Peter Arno and others. 183pp. 5⅜ x 8½. 22410-4

YEKL and THE IMPORTED BRIDEGROOM AND OTHER STORIES OF YIDDISH NEW YORK, Abraham Cahan. Film Hester Street based on *Yekl* (1896). Novel, other stories among first about Jewish immigrants on N.Y.'s East Side. 240pp. 5⅜ x 8½. 22427-9

SELECTED POEMS, Walt Whitman. Generous sampling from *Leaves of Grass*. Twenty-four poems include "I Hear America Singing," "Song of the Open Road," "I Sing the Body Electric," "When Lilacs Last in the Dooryard Bloom'd," "O Captain! My Captain!"–all reprinted from an authoritative edition. Lists of titles and first lines. 128pp. 5³⁄₁₆ x 8¼. 26878-0

THE BEST TALES OF HOFFMANN, E. T. A. Hoffmann. 10 of Hoffmann's most important stories: "Nutcracker and the King of Mice," "The Golden Flowerpot," etc. 458pp. 5⅜ x 8½.                                                                                        21793-0

FROM FETISH TO GOD IN ANCIENT EGYPT, E. A. Wallis Budge. Rich detailed survey of Egyptian conception of "God" and gods, magic, cult of animals, Osiris, more. Also, superb English translations of hymns and legends. 240 illustrations. 545pp. 5⅜ x 8½.                                                            25803-3

FRENCH STORIES/CONTES FRANÇAIS: A Dual-Language Book, Wallace Fowlie. Ten stories by French masters, Voltaire to Camus: "Micromegas" by Voltaire; "The Atheist's Mass" by Balzac; "Minuet" by de Maupassant; "The Guest" by Camus, six more. Excellent English translations on facing pages. Also French-English vocabulary list, exercises, more. 352pp. 5⅜ x 8½.                                      26443-2

CHICAGO AT THE TURN OF THE CENTURY IN PHOTOGRAPHS: 122 Historic Views from the Collections of the Chicago Historical Society, Larry A. Viskochil. Rare large-format prints offer detailed views of City Hall, State Street, the Loop, Hull House, Union Station, many other landmarks, circa 1904-1913. Introduction. Captions. Maps. 144pp. 9⅜ x 12¼.                                        24656-6

OLD BROOKLYN IN EARLY PHOTOGRAPHS, 1865-1929, William Lee Younger. Luna Park, Gravesend race track, construction of Grand Army Plaza, moving of Hotel Brighton, etc. 157 previously unpublished photographs. 165pp. 8⅞ x 11¾.
                                                                                                                            23587-4

THE MYTHS OF THE NORTH AMERICAN INDIANS, Lewis Spence. Rich anthology of the myths and legends of the Algonquins, Iroquois, Pawnees and Sioux, prefaced by an extensive historical and ethnological commentary. 36 illustrations. 480pp. 5⅜ x 8½.                                                                            25967-6

AN ENCYCLOPEDIA OF BATTLES: Accounts of Over 1,560 Battles from 1479 B.C. to the Present, David Eggenberger. Essential details of every major battle in recorded history from the first battle of Megiddo in 1479 B.C. to Grenada in 1984. List of Battle Maps. New Appendix covering the years 1967-1984. Index. 99 illustrations. 544pp. 6½ x 9¼.                                                                        24913-1

SAILING ALONE AROUND THE WORLD, Captain Joshua Slocum. First man to sail around the world, alone, in small boat. One of great feats of seamanship told in delightful manner. 67 illustrations. 294pp. 5⅜ x 8½.                                  20326-3

ANARCHISM AND OTHER ESSAYS, Emma Goldman. Powerful, penetrating, prophetic essays on direct action, role of minorities, prison reform, puritan hypocrisy, violence, etc. 271pp. 5⅜ x 8½.                                                    22484-8

MYTHS OF THE HINDUS AND BUDDHISTS, Ananda K. Coomaraswamy and Sister Nivedita. Great stories of the epics; deeds of Krishna, Shiva, taken from puranas, Vedas, folk tales; etc. 32 illustrations. 400pp. 5⅜ x 8½.                    21759-0

THE TRAUMA OF BIRTH, Otto Rank. Rank's controversial thesis that anxiety neurosis is caused by profound psychological trauma which occurs at birth. 256pp. 5⅜ x 8½.                                                                                      27974-X

A THEOLOGICO-POLITICAL TREATISE, Benedict Spinoza. Also contains unfinished Political Treatise. Great classic on religious liberty, theory of government on common consent. R. Elwes translation. Total of 421pp. 5⅜ x 8½.                20249-6

# CATALOG OF DOVER BOOKS

THE STORY OF THE TITANIC AS TOLD BY ITS SURVIVORS, Jack Winocour (ed.). What it was really like. Panic, despair, shocking inefficiency, and a little heroism. More thrilling than any fictional account. 26 illustrations. 320pp. 5⅜ x 8½.
20610-6

FAIRY AND FOLK TALES OF THE IRISH PEASANTRY, William Butler Yeats (ed.). Treasury of 64 tales from the twilight world of Celtic myth and legend: "The Soul Cages," "The Kildare Pooka," "King O'Toole and his Goose," many more. Introduction and Notes by W. B. Yeats. 352pp. 5⅜ x 8½.
26941-8

BUDDHIST MAHAYANA TEXTS, E. B. Cowell and others (eds.). Superb, accurate translations of basic documents in Mahayana Buddhism, highly important in history of religions. The Buddha-karita of Asvaghosha, Larger Sukhavativyuha, more. 448pp. 5⅜ x 8½.
25552-2

ONE TWO THREE . . . INFINITY: Facts and Speculations of Science, George Gamow. Great physicist's fascinating, readable overview of contemporary science: number theory, relativity, fourth dimension, entropy, genes, atomic structure, much more. 128 illustrations. Index. 352pp. 5⅜ x 8½.
25664-2

EXPERIMENTATION AND MEASUREMENT, W. J. Youden. Introductory manual explains laws of measurement in simple terms and offers tips for achieving accuracy and minimizing errors. Mathematics of measurement, use of instruments, experimenting with machines. 1994 edition. Foreword. Preface. Introduction. Epilogue. Selected Readings. Glossary. Index. Tables and figures. 128pp. 5⅜ x 8½.
40451-X

DALÍ ON MODERN ART: The Cuckolds of Antiquated Modern Art, Salvador Dalí. Influential painter skewers modern art and its practitioners. Outrageous evaluations of Picasso, Cézanne, Turner, more. 15 renderings of paintings discussed. 44 calligraphic decorations by Dalí. 96pp. 5⅜ x 8½. (Available in U.S. only.)
29220-7

ANTIQUE PLAYING CARDS: A Pictorial History, Henry René D'Allemagne. Over 900 elaborate, decorative images from rare playing cards (14th–20th centuries): Bacchus, death, dancing dogs, hunting scenes, royal coats of arms, players cheating, much more. 96pp. 9¼ x 12¼.
29265-7

MAKING FURNITURE MASTERPIECES: 30 Projects with Measured Drawings, Franklin H. Gottshall. Step-by-step instructions, illustrations for constructing handsome, useful pieces, among them a Sheraton desk, Chippendale chair, Spanish desk, Queen Anne table and a William and Mary dressing mirror. 224pp. 8⅛ x 11¼.
29338-6

THE FOSSIL BOOK: A Record of Prehistoric Life, Patricia V. Rich et al. Profusely illustrated definitive guide covers everything from single-celled organisms and dinosaurs to birds and mammals and the interplay between climate and man. Over 1,500 illustrations. 760pp. 7½ x 10⅛.
29371-8

Paperbound unless otherwise indicated. Available at your book dealer, online at **www.doverpublications.com**, or by writing to Dept. GI, Dover Publications, Inc., 31 East 2nd Street, Mineola, NY 11501. For current price information or for free catalogues (please indicate field of interest), write to Dover Publications or log on to **www.doverpublications.com** and see every Dover book in print. Dover publishes more than 500 books each year on science, elementary and advanced mathematics, biology, music, art, literary history, social sciences, and other areas.